THE TALL TALE OF MAXWELL ANDERSON

THE TALL TALE OF MAXWELL ANDERSON

Steve Joyce

Matador
9 Priory Business Park,
Wistow Road, Kibworth Beauchamp,
Leicestershire. LE8 0RX
Tel: 0116 279 2299
Email: books@troubador.co.uk
Web: www.troubador.co.uk/matador
Twitter: @matadorbooks

ISBN 978 1788037 037

British Library Cataloguing in Publication Data.
A catalogue record for this book is available from the British Library.

Printed and bound in the UK by TJ International, Padstow, Cornwall
Typeset in 11pt Cambria by Troubador Publishing Ltd, Leicester, UK

Matador is an imprint of Troubador Publishing Ltd

MIX
Paper from responsible sources
FSC® C013056
FSC www.fsc.org

ACKNOWLEDGEMENTS

To my wife Pam for encouragement, support and love.

I am grateful to the following people for their encouragement and assistance:

Alison Bruce, Zoe Neville-Smith, Steve Mustill, Matthew Tokley, Debra Tofts, Veronica Longman, Martin Neville-Smith, Belinda Morris, Madeleine McNaught.

Very special thanks to Neal Morse and Radiant Records for kind permission to use Neal's song titles in this book.
www.radiantrecords.com

To contact the author please send an email to:

stephen.joyce27@gmail.com

Twitter: @stevejoyceautho

1

READY TO TRY

The atmosphere was tense and the mood was grim. The conversation dripped with a viscous, palpable sense of disappointment. All four people present were tense, eyeing each other uncomfortably, steeling themselves for recriminations. Careers and reputations were hanging by a thread, and for at least one participant, more was at stake. His country's government was not revered for tolerating failure by its operatives.

One of the men began to drive the discussion. A slightly rotund man, he was dressed in designer smart-casual clothes. Sunglasses sat unnecessarily on top of his thinning blond hair. He was sweating freely, the strain of the situation getting to him, uncharacteristically so. This irritated him; normally he prided himself on being able to stay cool under pressure. His ability to prevent others knowing his true feelings and motives usually ensured that he was devastatingly effective in his assignments. However, this situation was far from usual.

"This is a complete disaster. Are you sure, Aleksandr, that the mother could not be saved?"

"That is irrelevant, as you well know. Her survival was

not a mission priority, nor was it a responsibility of my government." The reply came from a man dressed in a crisp military uniform. He was irked by the over-familiar use of his first name. His preference was to be addressed much more formally. The Englishman knew that, of course; he was adept at discovering a person's weaknesses, and exploiting them to his advantage.

"Oh, for fuck's sake, Aleksandr. Don't hide behind that 'my government' crap. We all want the same thing, don't we? Surely, once the foetus was declared unviable - and we still haven't got an explanation for that - then the mother's survival would have salvaged something! What do you think, Doctor?"

The third man, long-haired and long-nosed, had been cruelly compared in his college days to an Afghan hound by the other students, and sometimes, even by one or two of the lecturers. He took a moment to consider the question, and spoke methodically and dispassionately.

"I am obliged to concur with the Comrade Colonel. The mother's death was regrettable, but compared with the loss of the child, relatively incidental. We can still learn things from the cadaver. I will run some tests. We may discover how to increase the probability that the next attempt will be successful."

Spittle flew as the blond man responded. "Oh, for Christ's sake. How can you be so cold about this? You know how much is at stake here! We must find out what went wrong, and quickly. There's no point even thinking about the next attempt until we have a full explanation. And it has to be said, Doctor, that your inability to deliver results is now a matter of extreme concern for us."

The Russian said, “I am sure that if we all stay calm, a solution will soon present itself. Our mutual interests are far too significant to allow emotional petulance to get in the way of cool decision making.”

The fourth figure observed silently, curling her fingers in her long auburn hair. Abruptly, she stood up, commanding attention from the rest of the room.

“I’ve heard enough of this,” she said, with steel. “We’ve wasted enough time. Colleagues, I am initiating Project Scorpio. We have identified a suitable subject. You know of course what this means.”

The doctor nodded his silent acquiescence. The blond man stared at the woman, jaw-dropped and horrified. He was only too aware of the consequences of this announcement, for him personally, and people he cared about. Surely there was no need, just yet, to take this decision?

“You have a duty,” the woman reminded him, sensing his reluctance. After a few seconds’ contemplation, he inwardly accepted that his wider responsibilities must take precedence over personal considerations. He was fond of the Star Trek adage, “the needs of the many outweigh the needs of the few – or the one”. It was time to put this into practice.

“Project Scorpio is good to go. You can count on me.”

Quietly, the Russian military man uttered one word. “Finally”.

2

THE CREATION

When Mark Anderson climaxed on that fateful January morning, his perspiring wife Melanie flushed and breathless under him, he had no way of knowing that this simple act of lovemaking would give him fame and fortune, at a terrible, life-ruining cost.

In fact, at such delicate moments Mark was rarely aware of anything except the names of Formula One racing drivers, which he always frantically tried to recall to try and take his mind off things. This was seldom effective, and after years of employing this tactic, Mark found that in addition to slightly spoiling the final passion throes, he now felt a slight warmth and awkwardness whenever he watched a Grand Prix on TV.

"That was... nice", smiled Melanie as Mark, spent, rolled over onto the moist sheet, feeling damned with faint praise. 'Nice' was not exactly a glowing tribute to his lovemaking prowess.

"Thank you, darling", he replied. They always exchanged the same polite gratitude, which he felt to be faintly ridiculous given the nature of the act which preceded it.

"I think that was the one. I can feel it." Melanie stroked her abdomen tenderly.

"Darling, I hope so. I gave it my all."

Now in their fifth year of marriage, they had been trying to start a family for about a year. Separately and privately, they were each beginning to worry, and were plucking up courage to suggest to each other that fertility treatment should be attempted. Melanie was putting this off, frightened of discovering that her own reproductive capability was impaired; Mark was embarrassed about the testing process he would need to undergo. The thought of having to enter a cubicle with an empty glass phial and porn mag filled him with horror.

Inside Melanie, something wonderful began: a new life sparked into existence.

3

LOVE SHOT AN ARROW

Mark, now thirty-two years old, was average in almost every respect – his father would rather unkindly say "mediocre". His childhood was spent in a nondescript housing estate in an anonymous small town in the East Midlands, growing up with his sister Marie, younger by three years. His father, Roger Anderson, worked for a commercial insurance broker that enjoyed stable, unspectacular prosperity. Once or twice Roger would get a reasonably large Christmas bonus, and the family would enjoy a slightly more extravagant holiday the following summer. Roger's interests were modest; a model railway constantly being redesigned and rebuilt; every Thursday night out playing skittles at the Duke of York; and he spent every Sunday absorbed with a certain right wing broadsheet, cursing his way through the cryptic crossword. Tall, slightly overweight and suffering premature baldness, Roger never seemed content with his lot, and rarely showed much interest in Mark or Marie.

Mark's mother, Shirley, worked tirelessly to run the house and keep the family well fed and in clean clothes. She was a devout woman, attending Evensong, and cleansed her soul volunteering for Church fundraising activities, jumble sales (the same useless clutter endlessly recirculating) and the annual Spring Fayre. Mark never understood why "Fayre" was spelt with a "y": to attract more people, OBVIOUSLY, his father was always fond of saying.

Mark grew older without excelling either academically, on the sports field or in the music room or gymnasium. He was a 'second set' student and was the sort of boy that the teachers would not be able to remember a year or two after he left school. He inherited his father's height and but thankfully not the portly frame; Mark was thin and wiry, brown hair, brown eyes, not ugly but not the sort to turn heads either.

Mark graduated from secondary school with five O Levels, and began an unspectacular career in the Inland Revenue. As is typical in the Civil Service, Mark received a modest promotion every few years, whenever it was his turn. It was at work that he met Melanie, a freckly, red-haired girl one year his senior and one grade his junior. It was their shared interest in animals that drew them together; their first date was at Twycross Zoo. The trip was unforgettable thanks to an impromptu mating attempt by Gerald, the larger of the zoo's pair of bull giraffes, on his favourite female, Genevieve. Mark had thanked God aloud that he was not a female giraffe, which Melanie found wildly hysterical, and sealed the romance.

It also sealed her fate.

4

NOWHERE FAST

After a couple of years of marriage Mark and Melanie began to feel that their lives were falling into a rut. The same routine, day in, day out: the journey together to work, monotonous, subconscious and automatic; the working day spent in adjacent offices with the same colleagues, industriously collecting tax, never the most exciting of pursuits. And being civil servants, they never worked quite hard enough for the time to pass quickly. They always ate lunch together at the same sandwich bar; and rarely had conversation for each other during the drive home. Leisure time had become dominated by the television and using separate computers, she on Facebook, he playing online chess.

It was Melanie who spoke up first. "We're drifting, Mark, we need something more in our lives. Frankly, I'm getting bored."

"Are you thinking what I hope you're thinking, darling? Has the time come, at last?"

"Yes, my dear. I love you, Mark, but I need more. You're too important to me to allow our marriage to stagnate. We need to focus on something. We need to build for the future. We need to grow our family."

"You mean – are you saying – you'd like to have a –"

"PUPPY!" interrupted Melanie. "I want a dog! Oh, please say yes! We both like dogs and I've been looking into local breeders and rescue centres. It wouldn't cost very much at all and there's plenty of options. We've got plenty of places round here to walk a dog, we can get healthy raw food from the local butchers, and we can both apply for flexible working hours so the puppy isn't left too long. Let's do it!"

Mark and Melanie emptied the local library of dog books, carefully researching their choice of breed. Having chosen, they searched online to find a suitable breeder. They travelled to Cheshire to be interviewed by the breeder, a process Mark initially took exception to, until Melanie explained this is how reputable breeders ensure that their puppies go to the best homes.

Six months later, the Anderson collected their new family member, an eight week old Dalmatian puppy. They named him Matthew. Melanie had always been attracted to the idea of giving animals human names.

Melanie's yearnings for more were sated by Matthew's boisterous presence. The three of them became inseparable, even to the point of sharing a bed. "Our faithful four-legged contraceptive," as Mark would introduce Matthew to their rare visitors.

It was a few months past Matthew's first birthday, which had been celebrated with cards, parents, cake and the awkward embarrassment of singing 'Happy Birthday' to the dog. After relentless pressure from Mark's mother, Shirley (Roger had no strong desire to be a grandfather), and Melanie's parents, Robert and Belinda, or Bob and Bell as they called themselves, it was Mark who finally raised the possibility of starting a family. Melanie was happy to agree, not least because of the prospect of reinvigorating their sex life – but as joyful as it was to have Matthew bounding around, she had become all too conscious of the ticking biological clock, and had begun to want something more.

5

AUTHOR OF CONFUSION

"Mr and Mrs Anderson? The consultant will see you now." Mark and Melanie were in the waiting room of the Maternity Hospital, uncomfortably perched on impractically small, back-breaking plastic chairs. An hour beyond their allotted appointment, their initial nervousness had given way to boredom – celebrity gossip and caravanning magazines of no interest whatsoever to them – and boredom was fast being replaced by irritation. Three months pregnant and here for a routine scan, Melanie was tetchy.

"About time, too," she sneered at the receptionist, who recoiled in offence.

"Sorry about that. It's not your fault," soothed Mark, ever keen to avoid a scene.

They scuttled nervously into the consultant's office. Cramped, papers strewn across the desk, the badly decorated walls held shelves of aged, yellowing medical reference books, and dog-eared illustrations of embryos and foetuses at various stages of development.

Sat behind the desk was a podgy, middle aged man, about fifty, unkempt white tufts of hair either side of a bald, lumpy head. Narrow rectangular spectacles accentuated rather than disguised the man's close set eyes. A fat bulbous nose juxtaposed awkwardly over a small, tightly pursed mouth, itself out of place above two or three chins and a wobbly set of jowls. The man was dressed in a cheap, light grey suit that was slightly too small for him. Mark noticed food stains on the man's tacky Donald Duck tie.

"Good afternoon, Mark and Melanie – I'm Geoffrey Kelly, consultant paediatrician. I'll be looking after your family during the pregnancy – and subsequently." Mark was taken aback by the squeaky, effeminate voice, incongruous on such a bulky man. "First of all, may I humbly apologise for keeping you waiting so long. Quite unforgiveable."

"That's okay, we're here now," said Mark, but you really must get them to sort out some better magazines."

"I shall make it my first and most urgent priority, immediately after our meeting," replied Kelly, scribbling a note on a random piece of paper.

Kelly handed Mark and Melanie each a glossy A4 pamphlet entitled "Your pregnancy – what to expect."

"I would like to guide you carefully through the ante-natal care you'll be receiving. The first and important thing to remember is that I am here for you. Always and forever. If you need anything, anything at all, if you have any questions, concerns or problems, then please call me. This can be any time of the day or night – here is a card with my hospital mobile, personal mobile and home telephone numbers. Keep this with you at all times." Kelly handed over a cheaply printed business card, obtained from a station vending machine, Mark assumed.

Kelly continued, "I want you to know that I think you're a wonderful, special couple. Your baby is, and will be, the most important thing in your lives – and mine." Mark and Melanie exchanged a glance, him with raised eyebrow, her with a frown. Kelly continued, "I will do anything to help you." He affected a grin, attempting but not quite succeeding to be friendly and reassuring, like a creepy, over-familiar uncle.

Mark and Melanie shifted uneasily in their seats. There was something not quite right about this man, the over-earnestness and glint in his eye that made them wonder just what it was about them that was really so special.

6

NOTHING TO BELIEVE

The following Saturday, Mark and Melanie were sat awkwardly in Shirley's pristine living room. Everything was immaculate, as usual. At Mark's parents' house it was mandatory to remove one's shoes at the front door, a policy guaranteed to make visitors feel ill at ease.

Melanie was cradling a half-empty cup. The tea was far too milky for her tastes. It was irksome that Shirley did not make the effort to get this right. She was only drinking it to avoid causing offence, and would take out her frustration on Mark later.

"Would you like any more tea, dear?" enquired Shirley, unaware of her shortcomings in her efforts to appear an attentive host.

"No, I'm fine, thank you, Shirley," replied Melanie.

"How'd it go at the hospital?"

Mark said, "Oh, fine. Kept us waiting, typical NHS. Mr Kelly, our consultant, seems nice though."

"He gave me the creeps, and you too, Mark," said Melanie.

"Why, dear? What was the matter with him? I only hear good things about that hospital." Shirley frowned and looked attentively at Melanie. There's a chance of some gossip for the church ladies, she thought.

"Saw us an hour late, for a start. He was fat and scruffy. Egg stains down his tie. Office like a bomb site. You know what they say, you never get a second chance to make a first impression?" Melanie paused to take another ginger nut biscuit, careful not to drop a single crumb on the freshly vacuumed carpet.

"It wasn't that bad, Mel, he's obviously a busy man. You know what my desk looks like, and yours isn't exactly tidy," said Mark.

"That's not what you said at the time," she retorted, "but that wasn't the main issue. He was creepy. He was unctuous, ingratiating and smarmy. I didn't like him at all. And to think I have to let him rummage around in my privates." She shuddered.

"Oh, dear!" exclaimed Shirley, pulling a face at Melanie mentioning the 'unmentionables'.

Mark said, "I thought he was trying to be helpful. Trying to put us at our ease. He was a bit over the top, but I'm sure he means well. He wouldn't be holding down that job if he wasn't any good at it."

A door slammed, and Roger poked his head through the doorway. Evidently he had reached an impasse with his railway scenery painting. "Is there any more tea?" he asked Shirley. Shirley excused herself and followed Roger into the kitchen.

"Typical Dad. Far be it for him to offer to make some!" said Mark.

"Don't change the subject," hissed Melanie, "you're not being the perfect husband yourself at the moment. You could support me over this Kelly issue."

"I tried my best, darling. I rang the hospital and asked for a new consultant. I told you what they said – it's simply not possible. NHS cutbacks, they can't switch people around, you get what you're given. We have their best consultant as it is."

"They're just fobbing you off. You should have spoken to the Chief Executive."

"She wasn't available, and I did speak to the Clinical Director. If he says no, the Chief Exec isn't going to overrule him."

Melanie was not happy. "I've got a bad feeling about this, Mark. I don't feel comfortable with Kelly. I'm sure something will go wrong if we don't get this sorted out."

If only they had listened to the warnings screamed at them by Melanie's intuition, Mark would later come to bitterly regret.

7

THE PROMISE

Mark and Melanie made several more phone calls to the maternity hospital. Neither the Clinical Director or Chief Executive would change the stated position. Geoffrey Kelly was their best man, they said, and it simply isn't possible to allocate another consultant.

When they went to the hospital for Melanie's first tests and scans, they were anxious. Surely Geoffrey Kelly would know of their requests to change him? He's bound to be obnoxious now – and certainly won't be giving us his best care, Melanie had said. And being tense was hardly conducive to an easy gynaecological examination.

In fact, Kelly was, if anything, more charming than on their first encounter. He was gracious and respectful, and betrayed no awareness of the Andersons' attempts to replace him.

He calmly explained the various tests and procedures that Melanie would undergo, and patiently answered their questions. He regularly emphasised his commitment to them personally, and repeated his insistence that he was available at any time to provide support.

During Melanie's first examination, Kelly was gentle,

caring and worked unhurriedly, making sure that the mum-to-be was comfortable with each step in the process.

Scans showed that everything was normal, Kelly said reassuringly, all was proceeding exactly as you would expect. Mark and Melanie cherished the grainy ultrasound images, and showed them repeatedly to friends, family and colleagues, regardless of their level of interest.

Subsequent visits were similarly positive and uncomplicated, and as Melanie's pregnancy progressed, the couple became increasingly comfortable with Kelly, and excited about the coming addition to their family. At six months, after much debate, they decided to ask Kelly to tell them the gender of their baby. Kelly was only too pleased to extract a tiny tissue sample, although Melanie had winced when she saw the size of the needle he used to extract it. Fortunately, the local anaesthetic worked well.

In his now familiar effeminate tone, Kelly had said, "Mr & Mrs Anderson, I'm delighted to tell you that you will soon become the proud parents of a beautiful bouncing baby boy."

Mark and Melanie were both thrilled with this news – although they would have been with the alternative. With only twelve weeks to go, detailed preparations began in earnest. The spare bedroom was converted to a nursery, painted blue and adorned with luminous dinosaurs. Boy nappies were stockpiled, and suitable baby clothes obtained. The light blue romper suit emblazoned with the slogan "Hello, I'm new here" was Mark's favourite. Most importantly, the question of names was tackled. Mark and Melanie listed their principal family members' names: fathers, grandfathers, uncles; favourite film stars, music artists. The arguments then began in earnest and one by one the candidate names were eliminated. For want of a better selection method, a shortlist of ten names was then read out to Matthew, as he had developed quite an affinity with the bump, most evenings spent with head resting on Melanie's belly. Matthew's tail wagged the most for the tenth name read out.

"Well, that's settled then, darling," said Mark – "our son will be called 'Maxwell'. My granddad would be proud".

"Mark, Melanie, Maxwell and Matthew – that's charming, I love it," said Melanie, "What a happy family we shall make!"

This time, Melanie was mistaken. They had absolutely no idea how badly wrong. And by this time, the tissue sample extracted by Geoffrey Kelly was being analysed, molecule by molecule, in a laboratory thousands of miles away.

8

HEAVEN SMILED

Melanie woke with a jolt, distressed by a nightmare about being stabbed by a street robber. Blinking away her disorientation, in confusion that her mugger was nowhere to be seen, the agonising pains in her abdomen became a vivid reality. She glanced across at the digital clock, red numerals displaying 03:07. Mark was sleeping soundly, as usual. He always claimed to be a light sleeper, in marked contrast to the facts.

A deep stabbing sensation coursed through Melanie's lower body, and she let out a ghostly, ethereal moan. She jabbed Mark hard in the ribs. "Mark, it's happening. Get up!"

Mark's eyes widened as he took a few moments to comprehend. Melanie was writhing, arching her back as best she could with the distended globe of flesh she was carrying. "Jesus Fucking Christ, Mark, it's happening! Get up get up oh my God! Ambulance!"

As though suddenly plugged into the mains, Mark jolted upright and snatched the smartphone from the bedside table. As soon as the ambulance was summoned he pulled on yesterday's clothes, wincing each time Melanie let out a scream.

"Oh shit. Breathe deep, Mel, remember what Geoffrey told you. The ambulance is coming. Shit shit SHIT!"

They had, in fact, prepared meticulously for this. Melanie's suitcase was packed and ready in the hallway. Both smartphones were fully charged, and all conceivably relevant apps installed. Kelly has reassuringly explained that labour would be a gradual process, with plenty of time to reach hospital before serious pain began. Appropriate sedation and analgesic relief could be administered in order to avoid the worst discomfort, he had said. There was no need to worry.

In this respect, Kelly had got it badly wrong. The evening before, which marked the beginning of week thirty-seven, Mark and Melanie had spent a pleasant evening at their local Italian restaurant. She had gorged on black olives, satisfying one of several cravings that had provided infuriation and amusement in equal measures during her pregnancy. Other than Melanie's size and the expected swollen ankles, there had been no indications that labour was imminent.

Now, in the early hours, Melanie's condition deteriorated, the screaming became constant and more forceful. Mark gasped with relief when electric blue light flashed through the window, signifying the ambulance's arrival. Twelve minutes – not bad.

The neo-natal paramedic administered emergency pain relief and oxygen to Melanie, and within a few minutes the ambulance hurtled through the night. The emergency team was ready for them on arrival and Melanie was whisked straight into the delivery room. Before the door was shut in Mark's face, he glimpsed several masked figures clad in green coveralls, and saw the flashing lights of the attendant medical equipment. Absurdly, in spite of the situation and Melanie's continued howling distress, Mark thought of the Monty Python sketch about the machine that goes 'ping!'

A firm hand clamped his shoulder from behind, and the familiar high pitched voice of Geoffrey Kelly said, "Don't worry Mark. Your wife is being cared for now. Maxwell will soon be with us."

"Why didn't you tell us it would be like this? We had no warning! Mel's in such terrible pain – that's not what you said would happen!"

"Occasionally, Mark, there's a last minute complication. Your family will receive the best attention."

"Can I be with her? She can't go through this alone!"

"I'm afraid not. The doctors need space to work without being impeded." A ghastly, full-blooded scream pierced the room, causing Mark and Kelly to turn suddenly towards the theatre door.

"I've got to get in there! Something's wrong!"

Kelly looked Mark squarely in the eye and said, matter-of-factly, "The baby will be saved – at all costs. The best thing you can do is pray that delivery will be swift."

When Mark reflected back on this moment, he realised that Kelly's use of the word "delivery" was ambiguous.

A blood-curdling shriek filled the air. Mark went for the door but was held back by Kelly's vice-like grip. The two struggled but Mark was no match for the consultant's steely determination not to allow the birth to be disturbed. Abruptly, the screaming stopped.

"What's happening now?" demanded Mark. "How's Mel? How's the baby? I need to know what's going on!"

The door slowly opened. A tall, masked figure emerged,

green-suited, spattered in crimson blood. He was breathing rapidly, but despite the obvious exertion, he was pale, white as ice. He said, muffled through the mask, "Mr Anderson? I'm Doctor Crowe. Your son has been safely delivered. There were complications. I'm terribly sorry, but there was nothing we could do for your wife." Geoffrey Kelly nodded imperceptibly, lips pursed, as if trying to suppress a smile.

"What-what are you saying? Is Melanie OK? What's going on? Geoffrey, what's happening?" Mark burst past Kelly and Crowe and charged into the delivery room. A few green-robed, red-splashed figures were clustered in the corner, bent over a cot. A baby was cooing and gurgling. Across a metal trolley were strewn several bloodied tools, forceps, scalpels, scissors of various sizes. On the bed, contorted in death, lay Melanie, her face frozen in rictus agony, her abdomen and pubic area a mess of gore. No attempt had been made to conceal the ravages to his wife's body. Her eviscerated bulk had been sliced in an inverted Y configuration, the folds of flesh pulled open to reveal the gaping maw that had been her uterus.

"My God, you ripped it out of her. What did you do? WHAT DID YOU DO?" Mark rushed towards the corner, barging the medical staff out of the way. Mark saw his son for the first time.

Maxwell Anderson had a full head of sandy hair. He had the full complement of limbs, fingers and toes. He was breathing, contentedly sucking the third and fourth finger of his right hand. In every important respect, a normal, healthy baby boy.

Every important respect, that is, but one. Maxwell was tiny. About six inches long, he was about a third of the size of a baby born at thirty-seven weeks. Something was badly wrong.

"What the Hell has happened here?" asked Mark, of no-one in particular, but his voice tailed off into a whimper as the room seemed to physically spin around him. At once he felt weightless and yet crushed by the force of a suffocating weight pressing on his head, like being on a theme park's Pirate Ship. He whooped for air like a drowning man bursting through the surface of an angry ocean. "What's happening? What's happening?" he gasped.

Once again, Geoffrey clamped his hand on Mark's shoulder. He moved his jowly head close to Mark's and faintly whispered, "Something wonderful, Mark. Something wonderful."

9

WEATHERING SKY

The baby was kept in the maternity hospital for the first two weeks of its life while Mark put Melanie's affairs in order and held the funeral. Bob and Bell were devastated, naturally, and it fell to Roger and Shirley to make most of the arrangements. Roger, surprisingly enough, was a tower of strength to Mark, who couldn't recall ever receiving such good fatherly support; a source of some small solace amidst the overpowering tragedy of his wife's brutal death.

Melanie's autopsy results stated that she had died of a massive cardiac arrest while attempting to deliver her baby. Still numb, Mark struggled to reconcile the official cause of death with what he had seen in the delivery room. But for now his immediate attention was on sorting the officialdom that comes with a loved one's premature death. They had had the foresight to make wills, leaving all assets to each other; and Mark was the named beneficiary in Michelle's civil service pension. In the circumstances, the paperwork was as straightforward as could be expected.

Mark spoke with Geoffrey Kelly by telephone every day and received almost identical assurances each time. On the tenth or eleventh day, Kelly said, "Your son is doing very well

Mark, and is in safe hands. There's nothing to worry about. My colleagues have taken quite a shine to young Maxwell."

"What about his size? Is he growing?"

Kelly avoided the question. "He's fine and healthy, Mark. That's all you need to be concerned with."

Melanie's family were not particularly religious so the funeral consisted of a short, simple ceremony at the crematorium, followed by a wake at Bob and Bell's house. Bell was inconsolable, and disappeared upstairs soon after the wake began. Mark arranged for Melanie's favourite music to be played, 1980s pop – Duran Duran, Howard Jones, Soft Cell. "Say Hello, Wave Goodbye" triggered the most tears. There was even a lump in Roger's throat.

Two days after the funeral, Mark steeled himself to begin the next phase of his life – fatherhood. He began the twenty minute drive to the maternity hospital, unprepared for the shock he was about to receive.

10

REJOICE

It was pitch black and bitterly cold, as the four operatives assembled at their designated rendezvous point. The warmth of their greetings soon dispelled the chill.

The rotund blond beamed at his colleagues, his breath misting about him like steam from a locomotive. "We did it, Aleksandr!"

The Russian flinched at the informality, but allowed himself the flicker of a small smile. "Indeed. The project is proceeding acceptably within the mission parameters, at this very early stage."

"Oh come on, Aleksandr, live a little! We've cracked it this time, I can feel it!"

"Perhaps," said the third man, his long nose reddened and dripping in the frosty air, "the Comrade Colonel is right to be cautious. Things could still go wrong. I must admit though, I feel more optimistic about this attempt than I've ever done before."

"Let's stay focused," said the female agent, "we're here to ensure that the arrangements for the next phase are absolutely watertight. We've done well, but the hard work starts now."

"Yeah, and I still don't see why we couldn't do this online. Haven't the higher-ups heard of Skype? It's very inefficient to get together in person like this."

The blond man was teasing her, of course. They were all fully aware of the need for absolute secrecy, and of avoiding any digital trail of their plans. The repercussions of any breach would be severe. Even in this hi-tech era of data encryption and the dark internet, there was still no bullet-proof substitute for a clandestine meeting in a remote lay-by.

11

SO MANY ROADS

Geoffrey Kelly and Doctor Crowe greeted Mark in the hospital foyer. Kelly was wearing his usual ill-fitting suit, buttons straining against the weight. Out of his mask and robes, Crowe was surprisingly young, mid-thirties, long greasy hair tied into a pony tail, swarthy complexion and angular pointed nose. The open necked blue shirt clashed with mustard yellow trousers, an outfit more suited to the golf course than the workplace. They began to make small talk with Mark, his journey, the weather, and that he was looking so well, considering.

"I'm here to collect my son. I don't want to spend any more time in here than I absolutely have to." Mark wondered why Kelly and Crowe did not acknowledge the tragedy that had befallen him last time he was at the hospital – surely, the most harrowing and appalling experience a husband and father could possibly have.

"Of course, Mr Anderson," said Crowe.

They led him to a private room at the end of a grey, dimly lit corridor. A fifty-something nurse greeted Mark, her kindly expression marred by the beginnings of a bristly moustache. She led him to the cot beneath the window at the far end of the room. He peered into the cot, eager to look upon his son, eager to hold him in his arms.

Mark stifled a sharp intake of breath and held his hand to his mouth. "What's this? Is this a joke? There's been a mistake. Where's my son? What's going on?"

The fact that Max was naked was the least surprising thing Mark noticed. Lying on his back, Max was grinning and waving his arms, sandy hair all tousled, and beginning to darken. Mark was shocked and appalled to discover that his baby son was still only six inches long. Despite sixteen days having gone by since he had last seen him, Max had apparently not grown by even the slightest amount.

Kelly said, "Mark, there's something you need to understand. Your son is apparently healthy in every respect. We do, however, appear to have a most unusual phenomenon on our hands. Specifically, a remarkable case of dwarfism."

Mark looked at Kelly, mouth agape, struggling to take this in. "What do you mean?"

It was Crowe who continued. "As you will have realised, young Maxwell's birth size was significantly smaller than the average baby; approximately 70% smaller. This could signify some unusual circumstances during the pregnancy, for example, the mother drinking and smoking irresponsibly," he paused as Mark vigorously shook his head, "but as we know, Mr Anderson, through discussions with Geoffrey here, both yourself and Mrs Anderson were quite responsible parents."

Mark felt as though the room was lurching; he was back on the Pirate Ship.

"Oh yes," said Kelly, "they were model parents. Melanie didn't touch a drop for the whole thirty-seven weeks. And she'd never smoked."

"Never," said Mark, "but why hasn't Max grown?"

"I was coming to that," said Crowe. "An unusually small baby, if they survive the first few days, would ordinarily begin to grow, and by the third week, which is where we are now, you would perceive some modest difference – an inch or two. Rather surprisingly, your son is exactly the same size as when he was first born. We've conducted some tests, and have reached an empirical conclusion."

"What's happened," said Kelly, "is that young Maxwell has been born without the genetic and hormonal capabilities to grow. Although otherwise healthy, and as you can see, quite happy, he's trapped in a body that will not develop beyond the size of an average toy doll."

"How can you be so sure of this so soon? Perhaps he's just a late developer?"

"There's no doubt about the diagnosis, Mark. We're lucky in that Doctor Crowe here is a leading expert in this particular aspect of paediatrics. He has published several papers on dwarfism, gigantism and growth genes."

Crowe cut in. "The problem we have, Mr Anderson, is that Maxwell's brain is the only part of him that is growing. It is beginning to push against the skull's internal structure. Within a few days, this will cause irreversible damage to the brain – and probably, a quite painful death. We must act."

A feeling of dread and despair came over Mark, a cold icy grip. "What do you mean, 'act'? Kill him? I will not have him euthanized, like some diseased puppy! That's inhuman!"

"Please be calm, Mark," said Kelly, "That's not what we're talking about. There is a way to save baby Max. Doctor Crowe has a possible treatment in mind..."

"...I can cure Maxwell, Mr Anderson," said Crowe.

"There's a new gene treatment that can stimulate growth. It's still being tested, it's not licensed, it's not authorised - but I believe it can be effective in this case."

"Doctor Crowe is part of the development team for this new treatment," explained Kelly. "It's a remarkable breakthrough, a work of genius. It has the potential not only to end conditions such as dwarfism in humans, but its wider applications could change the world. Plant growth, animal growth, tree growth - the engineering Doctor Crowe has pioneered could alleviate many of the world's problems - such as hunger."

"Modesty forbids me from claiming the credit, but Geoffrey is basically correct. The team is on to something special. But we need to take the step from theoretical development and laboratory analysis to a practical, tangible demonstration of what this treatment can achieve. We need a human test subject. We need your son. It really is the only way of saving him. And there's no time to lose. We just need your written authorisation, and indemnity waiver, naturally."

Mark gazed into the eyes of the doctor, then Kelly, the nurse, and finally into the eyes of his baby son. The son that had already cost him his wife. Her life must not be in vain, he thought. The boy must survive at all costs.

"What's your answer, Mark?" asked Kelly, "will you give your son a chance to live?"

Mark took three deep breaths, his gaze not wavering from the tiny pink bundle writhing contentedly in the cot.

"Let's do it," he said. "Where do I sign?"

12

OH TO FEEL HIM

Roger and Shirley were waiting for Mark when he brought Max home for the first time. Bob and Bell were there, too, and even Mark's sister Marie had made the effort. But the most enthusiastic welcome came from Matthew, tail whipping like a rope in a storm, whining and whirling like a washing machine on fast spin.

"Hello, dog, did you miss me, did you miss me? Daddy's home! And look who's come to stay!"

It was a week since Mark signed the consent forms, authorising Doctor Crowe to experiment on Max. In that time Mark had begun a phased return to work. His manager, a huge, imposing woman called Lisa Plummer, had been most sympathetic and was affording Mark maximum flexibility. There were distinct advantages of working in the Civil Service; the pay was mediocre, but this was balanced by things such as family-friendly personnel policies.

Mark embraced his mother, then Marie, Bob and Bell in turn. His father confined himself to a brisk handshake. "How are you, son?" he asked, rhetorically.

Of course the main attraction was baby Max, whom all but Mark was meeting for the first time. Shirley and

Bell jostled to be the first grandparent to cuddle the new addition to the family. The baby comments came think and fast.

"Oh, he's gorgeous!"

"What a fine head of hair!"

"He looks happy!"

"He's a bonny lad, and no mistake!"

"But he's so…tiny!"

"He's got Melanie's eyes." That was Bell, and the atmosphere turned melancholic for a moment. Matthew, sensing the mood, or perhaps jealous of the attention Max was getting, let out a bark and dropped a ball, inviting someone to play.

Crowe and Kelly had attempted to explain the treatment to Mark, but their inability to express it in terms other than technobabble meant that Mark was pretty much in the dark even now. In essence, the procedure consisted of the insertion of synthesised proteins and hormones into the brain, spinal column and pituitary gland. Crowe had personally carried out the operation, assisted by Kelly, an anaesthetist and two or three nurses. Because Max's body was still so tiny, the incisions required were small, and in later life the scars would be barely perceptible. Drugs were administered to ensure that the baby's body accepted the artificial cells. A few days of careful monitoring completed the process.

During those few days, Maxwell Anderson doubled in size, to about 12 inches long.

13

THAT WHICH DOESN'T KILL ME

"Finally."

The man opened his eyes as the bolt on his cell door was drawn back for the last time, the metallic clank echoing around the block. Dozens of envious eyes drilled into him like lasers. He gave a silent prayer of thanks to his current chosen god.

To those who knew him before the trial, one of the most surprising things about the case was that the jury had judged him 'sane'. Shunned by neighbours and with no known friends, he had been thought of as distinctly weird and unpleasant. On the rare occasions he was seen outside, people were unsettled by his all-black attire including three-quarter length leather greatcoat with sinister Aryan overtones, augmented by his long straight white-blond hair and piercing pink eyes. He had a thousand-yard stare, disconcertingly giving an impression of being unhinged and calculating.

He regarded his incarceration, a seven-year sentence of which he had served half, as a tolerable inconvenience. The conviction, for stalking and cyber-terrorism offences, merely shifted his centre of operations to a new locale. He was able to continue formulating his ideology from the prison cell, storing all of the mantra inside his head. He had no need to store this digitally; in fact the electronic evidence he had produced in the past had led to his imprisonment.

He had used his time inside productively, undetected. As much as he could have continued this work from within the walls of Leicester prison, he was glad to be released today. Even more could be achieved in the outside world.

As he was led through the block towards the processing room, he exchanged exultant glances with many other prisoners, watching intently from their cells, some on the ground level, some on the upper level. These were Followers that the man had surreptitiously recruited, and some were unaware of each other's existence. The man had gained the allegiance of his Followers with craft, cunning and guile. Selecting those most likely to be susceptible to persuasion, the man secured their devotion initially though generosity with sexual favours, a powerful currency in prison. Over time, he was able to supplant this with motivational teaching and indoctrination.

The man left the block with a feeling of warm satisfaction. This time had been well spent.

14

THE LAND OF BEGINNING AGAIN

Slowly, life started to return to some semblance of normality for Mark. He returned to full time work, and received much sympathetic attention from his colleagues. Lisa had created the conditions for Mark to be treated as normally as possible. A replacement for Melanie had been discreetly recruited, a twenty-seven year old woman called Julie Patterson. She was pleasant, shy, slender and attractive. Mark liked her.

Childcare and dog-sitting duties were shared by the two sets of grandparents. Mark had taken care to ensure as even a split between them as possible, to avoid accusations of favouritism. It was particularly important for Bob and Bell to be included; they were grieving the loss of their daughter. The new baby gave them some focus, and took their mind off things to a small degree.

Max had a weekly check up with Geoffrey Kelly at the maternity hospital. Sometimes Doctor Crowe sat in on the session, but not always. Max continued to be healthy, and the alarming burst of growth in that first post-treatment week had slowed down to a healthy, normal rate.

Despite having to share attention with the baby,

Matthew took an immediate shine to Max. Each night he curled up to sleep next to the cot, and was constantly next to Mark when he was looking after Max, be it nappy changing, feeding, bathing or dressing.

Mark even found opportunities to resurrect his social life; a few beers and a curry with his oldest friend, Freddie Abbott. They had met at secondary school, at Dungeons & Dragons club; they soon bonded over common interests such as video games, 1970s progressive rock, and certain members of the girls' hockey team. Freddie was now earning a handsome living as a classic car dealer. He was divorced from one of the hockey team in question, and was currently attempting to live a playboy existence, punctuated by trips abroad. Despite the divergent paths their adult lives had taken, Mark and Freddie remained very close friends. Freddie had been best man at Mark and Melanie's wedding. Mark told Freddie that if Max had been christened, Freddie would be the first choice as godparent. However, in deference to Melanie's family's agnostic viewpoint, no christening would take place.

Freddie would be a tower of strength for Mark in the difficult years ahead.

15

LEVIATHAN

"....Happy Birthday dear Max-well, Happy Birthday to you!"

Max's first birthday party was held at Roger and Shirley's house. Bob and Bell did not attend, Bell was too upset on this, the anniversary of their daughter's death. Bob was busy pursuing a campaign against the hospital to force them to explain how it was that giving birth to a tiny baby could have caused such a catastrophic reaction in Melanie's body. Bob was sure that negligence must have contributed to her death, and the hospital was protecting its employees. His attempts to meet with Geoffrey Kelly and Richard Crowe had been met with bureaucratic rebuttal. Mark felt that had Bob realised the extent of the physical mutilation her body had suffered, he would doubtless have embarked on a very public and vociferous crusade for justice. Mark had chosen not to reveal the truth to his wife's parents, sensing that this would utterly destroy any chance they would have had of coming to terms with her untimely passing.

It was a small gathering; Marie was on holiday with girlfriends, but had been considerate enough to send her good wishes by text message. Freddie came along for moral support; this was a difficult day for Mark, too. Completing the assembled throng was Geoffrey Kelly. During the past year, Mark had come to appreciate Kelly's patience and attention during the post-natal check-ups, and a relationship akin to that of a friendly uncle had built up.

Max was too young to appreciate the birthday wishes, or enjoy the cake, complete with teddy-bear icing. A supermarket special. Max's slice therefore went to Matthew, who devoured it in less than a second. "That didn't even touch the sides," observed Roger.

"When are you going to get the little man's haircut, Marky?" asked Freddie. "He's beginning to look like a girl. You don't want to give him an identity crisis so young, do you?"

Max gurgled playfully, seemingly aware that he was the cause of the warm feelings in the room.

"Mr Kelly, I have a question for you," said Shirley. "Don't you think Maxwell is a little big for his age?"

"Mrs Anderson, your grandson is a healthy boy. Other than the long hair, which I agree is not ideal for a young man, I see nothing out of the ordinary."

"But Mark tells us that every week he's having to buy new baby clothes. It's costing him a fortune."

"The baby's development is in line with normally accepted parameters, Mrs Anderson. Given how young Maxwell started out in life, it should be pleasing to see that progress is being made."

"How big is he now, then Marky?" asked Freddie.

"It's been a week or so since I measured him – hang on, I'll get the tape measure."

It took a few moments for Max to stop wriggling long enough for Mark to take a reliable measurement.

"Hang on, this can't be right," said Mark. "Let me try that again. Mum, hold him still, will you?" Mark repeated the process. "Good grief!" he exclaimed.

"What is it, Marky?"

"Well mate, my fine young son is now thirty-six inches long. Or high. That's four inches more than last week."

Roger said, "Thirty-six inches, are you sure? Shirley, get that baby book, will you?" Shirley reached for a dog-eared book from their shelf, the one her own mother had bought her when she was expecting Mark. There was an average height chart in the back of the book.

It showed that the average height for a 12 month old baby was 30 inches. Maxwell Anderson was about six inches bigger than Shirley's thirty-five year old book said he should be.

16

IN THE FIRE

"Ach, not again." Geoffrey Kelly slammed his computer mouse against the table. He was home, alone as usual. It was a little after eleven o'clock. He had just lost his fifth consecutive game of online poker and was sixty pounds down on the session so far. Still, plenty of time to win that back and make a profit. The online poker hall never closed.

He was still in his work clothes, apart from his tie and his shoes, which were dumped haphazardly in the hallway. It was a modest house; two up two down, end terrace. It was sparsely decorated, magnolia walls, no pictures or paintings. An olive green leather settee juxtaposed awkwardly against a dirty orange patterned carpet. There was a wooden rocking chair placed in front of a large plasma TV, the only extravagant item on display. Used plates and unwashed cups and glasses littered the room. All of this was intermittently illuminated by the flicking PC monitor – no lights were on. Kelly was trying to save a bit of electricity.

He started a new poker game, committing a ten pound ante. The deal was much more like it, he thought, lucky enough to get six, seven and eight of hearts in the same hand. A straight flush was there for the taking. He raised the bet by a further ten; one player folded but two others stayed in the game. He burned two cards and waited for the replacements. A rush of excitement coursed through his body: five of hearts and eight of clubs. The straight flush was on! Hang on though – a pair of eights – should he play safe and go for three of kind? His mind raced as a competitor upped the bet by ten more pounds. He was already twenty quid committed, but he couldn't back out now. What would give him the best odds of success? A four or nine of hearts would give him the straight flush –that's two cards out of the remaining pack. There were also two eights available –so an equal chance of getting a threesome. The straight flush was better – he burned the one black card in his hand.

Thousands of noughts and ones streamed through the cables as the program dealt his final card. He drained his whisky glass and felt a twinge of apprehension as he hovered the cursor over the back of the card. "Come on, come on. Four or nine of hearts. Four or nine," he muttered. He clicked the mouse and blood drained from his face. Jack of Diamonds. "Fuck it all anyway," he said, and prepared to fold.

Hang on a minute, he thought, I could bluff my way out of this. They don't know I've got a pile of shit. He raised the bet by twenty, one further player folded, leaving just one opponent. His bet was matched and raised by twenty more. Shit, thought Kelly, he's calling my bluff. Can't back out now. Fifty quid already on the line, and the other guy's probably bluffing anyway, he had already won two games that way.

He matched the bet and raised it by thirty more: a full ton of his money riding on this, but more to gain if he wins. Kelly was horrified to see his opponent match the bet and call. He went to swig some more whisky, but was irritated to find his glass still empty. He was obliged to reveal first, and the program impatiently prompted him to get on with it. With a click and a curse he revealed his hold card and the fact that he had absolutely nothing. The opponent instantly showed his full hand. The bastard had bluffed him out of a hundred quid with a measly pair of Queens.

The program silently and efficiently drained Kelly's account of the hundred pounds, making tonight's losses a hundred and sixty quid already. In fact, this added to the already gigantic size of Kelly's unauthorised overdraft. He owed the bank a frightening sum. He owed lots of money to lots of people, some of whom would come knocking any day now.

"I'll win this time," he chuntered, and refreshed his glass. "Deal, you digital dickhead," he said, and clicked the mouse to start a fresh hand.

17

IT'S ALL I CAN DO

Maxwell was three feet and nine inches tall on this third birthday; the size of an average six year old boy.

Mark had demanded answers from Geoffrey Kelly and Doctor Crowe. It was them who had diagnosed "a remarkable case of dwarfism" – almost funny now – and it was them who persuaded Mark – actually it felt like coercion – to submit his son to the unorthodox treatment that was now having such dramatic results.

His mother's comments at Max's first birthday party about the expense of replacing clothes were exaggerated then, but this had since become a serious problem. Baby clothes, and shoes, were frightfully expensive but Max had long outgrown these. Already too big for toddlers' outfits, Max was now getting through clothes designed for primary schoolchildren. Recently, Mark had resorted to charity shops and eBay bargains to keep the expense manageable.

This was not the only problem – Max had a voracious appetite. He was always famished, eating several meals a day but constantly mithering in between. It seemed that the only way to keep him happy was to put food in front of him. The strain this put upon Mark was immense, but the people who bore the real brunt were Max's grandparents, after all, it was them who did the bulk of the childcare during the working week.

And, not to put too fine a point on it, there was a consequence of eating so much, at the other end of Max's digestive tract. Although physically resembling a six year old, Max's mental development was apparently normal. He still had a toddler's intellectual capacity and behaviour. It was not possible to find disposable nappies in Max's size, so Mark had sourced a suitable towelling material and made his own nappies, washable. Potty training was not going well; the amount of laundry generated was therefore problematic – and expensive to process.

There was a particularly upsetting incident a few months after Max's second birthday. Mark's son was crying, hungry as usual. After a feed and a change Mark was hopeful for an hour or two's respite. No such luck: immediately Max began crying at a blood-curdling volume level. Mark tried various different food items – Max's favourites, bubble and squeak, apple puree, chocolate mousse – nothing would stop the shrieking. Mark decided to change the nappy again, and was horrified to discover that he had safety-pinned one of Max's buttocks to the towelling; a serious puncture wound had been suffered. Poor Max had been unable to communicate what was wrong except by screaming. Absolutely mortified, Mark cried his eyes out at the thought of the unimaginable pain he had inflicted upon his poor son.

Afterwards, Mark reflected that this was the first time he had cried since he lost his wife. It had taken Max's suffering to trigger an emotional release that was badly needed and long overdue.

It also crystallised in Mark's mind feelings he had been having for a while: firstly, that he wasn't really coping on his own despite all the help from Mum and Dad, Bell and Bob; his life was all work and Max. As importantly, he desired adult female companionship again.

It was time to put himself first, he had decided.

18

EVERYTHING IS WRONG

Meanwhile, the mystery of Max's growth rate was still unsolved. Kelly and Crowe were unable to provide any answers or explanations.

Nor were they prepared to initiate any physical intervention. "The problem, Mr Anderson," Crowe said, "is that with unproven medical technology, we cannot reliably assess the risks of interfering with what is now an embedded part of your son's genetic composition. The consequences could be disastrous."

"But you must have some idea. You're heading up the team that developed this treatment! What about your laboratory tests – and experiments on animals? Haven't you attempted a reversal before?"

"I'm not willing to share those outcomes with you, Mr Anderson. Suffice it to say that I would not have any confidence that we could avoid causing irreparable damage."

"But why didn't you foresee this problem? Why wasn't I warned that this might happen?"

"I am confident you will find, if you refer to the documentation you signed before the treatment began, that no written guarantees of any kind were given."

"You bastard, Crowe. I'll sue you and this bloody awful hospital!"

"Again, Mr Anderson, the indemnities you signed are fairly watertight. There would be no prospect of any successful claim being brought. You apparently accepted this at the time."

Geoffrey Kelly put a hand on Mark's shoulder, and in the most soothing tone he could muster, said, "Things aren't really so bad, are they Mark? You have a happy, healthy son. Yes, he's on the tall side, and I appreciate the practical difficulties. But there are thousands of parents who either can't have children, or have lost a baby to cot death, or are raising a child with debilitating mental or physical handicaps."

"Be thankful for what I have, you mean? There's always someone worse off than yourself? I don't need to be patronised, Geoffrey. I know that I'm lucky to have Max. But there's something weird happening to him and I want to know what it is."

Crowe said, "Your position is entirely understandable, Mr Anderson. I'm afraid that the best I can suggest is that we continue to monitor the boy's development. In my professional opinion, it's extremely unlikely that this abnormal growth rate will continue for much longer."

Whether Crowe was incompetent or simply lying, Mark had difficulty deciding when Max reached six feet tall when just four and a half years old.

19

I AM WILLING

Mark began dating Julie Patterson at about this time. He discussed the possibility of getting a new girlfriend with Roger and Shirley, worried about it being too soon. What would people think? His parents reassured him that a grieving period of over four years was more than enough, and no reasonable person would think less of him for getting on with his life. Mark didn't feel able to have a similar conversation with Bob and Bell, he was reassured to find out via Shirley some time later that he had Melanie's parents' full support. It was time to move on.

An embarrassing incident had finally galvanised Mark into getting back onto the dating wagon. Late one evening in the office, Mark was finishing a batch of paperwork when Lisa Plummer called him into her office.

"Sit down, Mark," she said and paused. Eventually, she said "I want you to know how much I respect the work that you do here."

"Er....yes, thank you, I do my best." It was not Lisa's usual style to give spontaneous praise like this. A perfunctory "well done" at the annual appraisal was all people had come to expect.

Lisa had continued, "And I also want you to know that I think you underestimate yourself. In particular, your value to me, personally, and your attractiveness, as a man." She perched on the edge of her desk and attempted a coquettish pose; this was neither a natural or aesthetically pleasing position for such a bulky woman to adopt.

The colour drained from Mark's cheeks, and he felt distinctly uncomfortable. How was he going to get out of this? "Lisa, I don't know what to say. I really like you as a boss, and will always be grateful for your support when Mel died. You're a good friend. But I don't want to risk spoiling what we have."

Fire flickered across Lisa's eyes. "Don't you find me desirable, Mark? We could be so good together. I'm a woman. You're a man. We're both available. How about it?"

"I don't think so, Lisa, it's me, not you, I just don't think of you in that way, I'm so sorry."

"Well, if that's the way you feel about it, you may go. See you tomorrow." Things were always awkward between them after that, Lisa was invariably moody and surly towards him. He considered making a complaint under the sexual harassment policy, but on balance decided that this would be a one way ticket for him out of the organisation. The Civil Service doesn't like troublemakers. Mark decided to keep quiet, although he realised that there would be no promotion opportunities from that moment forward.

As things turned out, he would experience a fame and fortune beyond what the Civil Service could deliver.

One month after the Lisa encounter, Mark asked Julie out for a lunchtime drink. She readily agreed, and the relationship blossomed quickly.

20

CHANCE OF A LIFETIME

Maxwell Anderson started attending primary school in September of that year, a month before his fifth birthday. Fortunately, toilet training was substantially complete by this time; only occasional accidents.

Of greater concern to Mark was the fact that Max was now six feet eight inches tall; towering over not just the children, but all the school staff as well.

He arranged a meeting with the headteacher, a week before school began. Mrs Taylor was in her forties, buxom, with long curly black hair and grey roots, and wore rather too much make up. She had a brisk, business-like manner that exuded empathy and calm authority.

Julie accompanied Mark to the meeting. They both wore their Sunday best, keen to make a good impression. Max and Matthew were being looked after by Bob and Bell that day. Julie stayed in the car when Mark dropped them off. She still felt awkward when dealing with Mark's dead wife's parents.

Mrs Taylor's office was spacious and clean. It looked recently decorated, walls pastel pink. A large landscape print of a Himalayan range adorned the wall behind her desk. A bookcase filled with volumes on management, parenting, sociology and psychology was on one side of the room; another wall displayed her professional qualification certificates. The layout was completed by a small round meeting table and chairs. On Mrs Taylor's desk were two slimline computer monitors, wireless mouse and keyboard, and a lever arch file labelled "OFSTED Inspection". This was going to be a busy term.

"Thank you for agreeing to meet with us, headmistress," said Mark. "What a lovely school you have here."

"It's always a pleasure to meet new parents, Mr Anderson. You may call me 'Mrs Taylor' – the term headmistress died out a long time ago. What can I do for you?" Straight to the point, no time wasted with small talk.

"My son starts here next week. He's nearly five."

"Yes indeed, we shall be delighted to welcome young Maxwell. He shall be in Miss Foster's class. One of our finest young teachers. The children adore her."

"She sounds very nice," said Julie.

"And all the mums like her, too, Mrs Anderson."

Julie reddened. "Oh, I'm not..."

"That's one of the reasons we want to see you, Mrs Taylor," said Mark. "This is Julie Patterson, she's a – friend. I'm afraid to say that there is no Mrs Anderson. Maxwell's mother died a few years ago."

"I'm very sorry to hear that, Mr Anderson. What a terrible burden for you to bear. And losing one's mother at a young age can be terribly destabilising for a young boy. I'm so glad you brought this to my attention."

"Actually, Max has no memory of his mother – she... she....sorry, this is difficult...she died giving birth to him."

"Oh, that's awful. I'm very sorry indeed, once again.

Please let me reassure you however, here at Southfields School we have a lot of experience of children without the full complement of parents, for whatever reason."

"That's good to know, thank you," said Mark. "There's something even more important you need to be aware of regarding my son." He paused; Julie gave Mark's hand a comforting squeeze.

"Whatever it is, Mr Anderson, I'm sure we'll cope. After many years of integration, we have become adept at managing a range of emotional and behavioural difficulties, physical handicaps, too. Obviously the severest cases still go to special schools."

"My son has an unusual physical condition, Mrs Taylor. It's a form of gigantism. He's been growing fast all of his life, and shows no sign of slowing down. He's currently six feet eight inches tall."

The headteacher raised her eyebrows and allowed her jaw to drop. After a few seconds she collected herself, and the mask of professionalism slid back into place.

"All sizes and shapes are welcome at Southfields. He will be a valued addition to our school, Mr Anderson. And, I imagine, quite a basketball player."

"We're worried about the possibility of bullying, Mrs Taylor. Kids who are different always get picked on."

"We have a zero tolerance policy on bullying and I promise to ensure that all staff look out for young Maxwell. No doubt we shall encounter difficulties, but I anticipate these will be mainly logistical. Many activities, especially physical education, will need to be adapted, but that's our problem to solve. Leave it to us, Mr Anderson, your son will be in safe hands here."

"Thank you," said Mark and Julie together.

"It was a pleasure meeting you, Mr Anderson. And Miss Patterson. See you next week." A firm handshake signified the end of the meeting.

"She seems very nice," said Julie.

"Yes, I suppose so," Mark replied. "I just want Max to have as normal a school life as possible. I think we've made a positive start today."

However, Mark and Maxwell's troubles were only just beginning.

21

NIGHTTIME COLLECTORS

It was a cold, misty evening. A silver Ford Mondeo, several years old, not the latest model, flashed its orange indicator and glided onto the motorway slip road. After a sharp braking manoeuvre (the bend always more severe than expected), the car entered the Corley services, a few miles near Coventry. It pulled into a parking space on the edge of the car park furthest from the shopping and restaurant building.

"Christ, this is a godforsaken place," muttered the driver, to no-one in particular. "Why can't we do this in a nice pub somewhere, for fuck's sake."

He killed the engine and switched off the headlights. Ten seconds later, he flashed the lights three times in quick succession. This was the pre-arranged signal. He sat back and waited, drumming his fingers on the steering wheel, feeling tense, irritated.

The dim overhead night lights lit up the mist surrounding the Mondeo, bathing it in an eerie luminescence, like a semi-transparent cotton wool. Realising his mistake, the man switched on the ignition and moved the car to a space that was not illuminated, in what was possibly the most desolate part of the site. The man recalled Luke Skywalker's statement: "If there's a bright centre of the universe, this is the place it's furthest from."

He flashed the headlights another three times and waited. Several more minutes passed, enough for the air in the car to get cold. The man's breath began to vaporise, clouding the windows with grey mist.

Three sharp knocks on the passenger side front window made him jump out of his skin. "Jesus Christ!" he exclaimed. The door opened and a younger man plonked himself into the passenger seat. In the few seconds before the interior light faded out, the driver saw that the newcomer was young, perhaps mid-twenties, with unruly hair and a goatee beard. He wore a leather jacket and leather gloves.

In a strong Birmingham accent, the young man said "Hey, you made it, nice one. You bring the stuff?"

"No, I left it on the kitchen table! Of course I've got it. Let's see the money."

"Just a second old man, let's see what you've got."

The older man reached behind the passenger seat and lifted through a small black briefcase. He twiddled the three-digit combination lock and flicked the case open. He pulled out a manila folder, and handed it across to his companion, who flicked through the contents. Documents, photographs, official looking forms. The younger man let out a short contented whistle.

Without averting his gaze, he retrieved a thickly padded envelope from his jacket pocket. "Count it," he said, tossing it over to the driver. Flicking through the bank notes, the older man said "It's all there."

"Hey, there's more where that came from, if the rest of the stuff is as hot as this."

"Oh, there's a lot of good material. I'll get it together. Shall I contact you in the same way?"

"You betcha. Thanks, old man."

"Will do. And I'll pick the drop off point next time – I don't want to come to this shit hole ever again."

"I'll be waiting." And with that, the younger man sprang out of the car, folder in hand, and disappeared into the night.

The driver fired up the engine and impatiently tutted while he waited for the windscreen to demist. He eased the Mondeo out of the car park, cursing as he realised that he would have to go up to the next junction and turn back on himself to return to his East Midlands home.

"I'm NEVER going to come to this place again," said Geoffrey Kelly, as he eased the Mondeo onto the main carriageway.

22

BREAK OF DAY

Max felt weird that morning. He knew he was going to do something really special. He was going to a big building called "Southfields School". At this place he was going to make some new friends, and play some new games. He was going to meet a nice lady called Mrs Taylor, and a REALLY nice lady called Miss Foster. Daddy said that Max would have a wonderful time, but he had this funny feeling in his tummy. Daddy called this "butterflies". Max knew what butterflies were, but he hadn't swallowed any, so he couldn't work out why any would be in his tummy. Daddy was silly, sometimes.

Julie was there, helping Max to get dressed. Max liked Julie. She was nice. She came round a lot, and always made yummy food. His favourite was "ravvy-olly".

"Now then Max, watch carefully," said Julie, This is how you do your shoelaces up." Max was sat on the edge of the bed, but paid no attention to what Julie was doing. He was too busy playing with his cuddly toy Brachiosaurus, named, inevitably enough, 'Brackie'. Brackie was his favourite toy; he was cool! Max had a dinosaur bedspread, dinosaur pillowcase, dinosaur posters on the wall. He had a dinosaur jigsaw – thirty thick wooden pieces, a cartoon brachiosaur eating leaves from a gigantic tree – dinosaur activity books.... and specially for today, Daddy and Julie had bought him a dinosaur pencil case AND a Brachiosaurus lunchbox! Max really wanted the dinosaur pyjamas he had seen in the shop, despite them featuring a stegosaur instead of his favourite – but he was too big for them. Makers of kiddie pyjamas hadn't expected to cater for strapping six-footers. Or seven-footers, for that matter.

Shoes tightly laced, Max was ready. He was wearing dark brown corduroy trousers, burgundy pullover, dinosaur rucksack and a black, custom-made, slimline crash helmet. He had now reached the height of not being able to fit through doorways. Unfortunately, his brain, still less than five years old, had not had enough time to get used to the idea of ducking when going through each door. Within recent weeks, Max had suffered several frightful accidents, hefty thuds of skull into doorframe that quite apart from the immediate concern for the appalling pain, had seriously worried Mark about permanent damage to Max's brain. He had sourced the helmet from an online supplier that specialised in safety equipment for epilepsy sufferers.

Mark was deeply worried about today. The helmet was unusual enough in itself to attract unkind comments from Max's new classmates, but this was clearly the least obvious of the physical attributes that would make his son stand out from the crowd – in more ways than one! Max would be about twice the height of most of the rising fives starting today. All Mark could do was hope that Mrs Taylor was as good as her word, and that Miss Foster would quickly intervene to halt the inevitable taunting.

"Can we go Daddy, can we go, Daddy can we go!"

Someone was getting excited. Julie sat with Max in the back of the people carrier, his head awkwardly pressed against the car roof, and Mark drove them to the school, parking around the corner. They walked towards the front gate, Max in the middle, adults on either side, holding his hands. Julie carried the Brachiosaurus lunchbox in her other hand.

Across the road, they noticed a huddle of three or four mums, and assorted offspring. In animated discussion, they were watching Max intently, one of them pointing.

"Here we go," said Mark.

"Ignore them," replied Julie, "they'd be like that with anyone new."

Max, oblivious to the attention, was singing the Wiggles theme tune.

A few cars went past, drivers gazing at them as they went past. Keep your eyes on the road, thought Mark, you'll run someone over.

As they neared the gate, the commotion grew a little more obvious. Children began laughing and pointing, parents held hands over mouths in shock. Max began to sense that the behaviour was directed towards him.

"What's wrong, Daddy? Why are people pointing at me?"

"There's nothing wrong, Max. They like your dinosaur bag, that's all."

"It's a rucksack Daddy, not a bag. And they can't have it – Brackie is cool. He's my friend. And he's mine!"

"There's Mrs Taylor," said Julie. The headteacher was just outside the school entrance, greeting all the new arrivals.

"Ah good morning, Mr Anderson. And Miss Patterson. And this must be young Maxwell! What a fine handsome young man. Welcome to Southfields School!" She offered her hand to Max. Confused, Max did not reciprocate, and tried to hide behind his father.

"I can still see you! Come on young man, let's go and meet Miss Foster, and get you started."

"You have my number should you need me – please call if you need to," said Mark.

"Please try not to worry, Mr Anderson, we'll look after Maxwell just fine." She turned her head up to Max – he was looking around the playground, wary, disoriented.

After confirming with the headteacher that the school had their emergency contact details, Mark and Julie said their cheerios to Max – "Have fun!" – and watched with worried eyes as Mrs Taylor took him by the hand and walked him into the innards of the school. As she did so, Max's helmet collided with the door frame, and off he went.

As Mark turned away, his attention fell upon a woman who was staring at them intently. She was crying. Mark assumed that she was distressed at Max's difference from the other children – aware of the potential for unhappiness this may cause. Some people were capable of compassion.

Outside the school gates, a young man with a goatee beard put his camera phone into his leather jacket inside pocket, turned away, and walked hurriedly towards a waiting black Range Rover, its engine purring impatiently.

23

IT'S FOR YOU

On the drive to work, Julie said, "He'll be fine, Mark. The other kids will soon get used to him."

"I'm sure you're right. I can't help worrying about him, though."

"That's completely understandable. Every parent must feel the same way when their kids start school."

"This is different. Max is different. He's so – vulnerable." Mark lifted a hand from the steering wheel to wipe a tear from his eye.

"I love you, Mark," said Julie, and she reached across to squeeze his thigh; at the next red traffic light, she leaned across and kissed his cheek.

Mark's smartphone beeped, signalling the arrival of a text message. "That didn't take long!" he said. Julie lifted the phone out of his shirt breast pocket and accessed the text message. "It's from Freddie – he says 'How'd it go Marky mate? – hope all went well. Thinking of you. Speak soon.' Ah, that's nice."

"Always been a good mate, Freddie," said Mark.

Freddie Abbott would come to justify that accolade many times over.

24

SO LONG GOODBYE BLUES

The woman looked at her reflection in the full length bedroom mirror.

She was naked.

Her eyes were raw from yet another bout of sobbing, her face and neck reddened from the exertion. A light moustache tainted her upper lip. She leaned forward and gazed closely at three spots on her chin, and idly fingered the jowly flesh underneath. A couple of thick, wiry hairs sprouted from a mole on her cheek. Her thinning, brown yet greying hair was unwashed, unruly and uncared for – the woman had not been to a salon for more than a year.

Looking down, she sighed at her ample, pendulous yet uneven breasts. She had large mottled nipples. She had always hated these heavy, uncomfortable objects. Tufts of unsightly armpit hair protruded. From a young age she had been afflicted by above average hirsuteness and brown hairs coated her arms. She had been called "Chewbacca" at secondary school.

Her abdomen was bulbous, her gut overhanging her pubic area. Years of comfort eating had swelled her figure to a size twenty-two, and she was disproportionately large around the stomach and hips area. Cradling her gut, the woman glanced at the mass of unkempt pubic hair. Still a virgin at forty-one, and no wonder, she thought, as she peered down at her blotchy, tree-trunk legs, fat ankles and podgy feet.

The woman began crying, and swallowed another measure of vodka from a half-empty bottle.

Her life had been difficult. Her parents had a dysfunctional relationship, always arguing. Though never violent, there had always been a tense atmosphere. When young, the woman had been denied pocket money and attractive clothes, but had been spoilt with vast quantities of unhealthy, lard-ridden food. She had been fat since primary school, and endured the taunting of unkind classmates until leaving school at sixteen.

At school there had never been boyfriends – she never felt attractive or confident enough to get close to anyone, and she had never been asked out. From taking a boring office job at work she had actually done reasonably well for herself through sheer hard work; fairly regular promotions had been conferred, and she had recently received a long service award for twenty-five years loyal contributions. She was not popular with her colleagues, especially those that she was responsible for. She had developed a crush on one of her staff, but this was very obviously not reciprocated. She had clumsily tried to act on her urges, but had been rebuffed. She was devastated.

Recently, there had been a potential chink of light among the gloom; only for it to end it yet another soul-crushing disappointment. An attractive young man had befriended Lisa on Facebook, having got to know each other on a 1980s pop music fan page. Their private online chats showing how much they apparently had in common, a love of Duran Duran, Heaven 17 and Go West in particular, many of the same movies, and they even liked the same food! Lisa had felt that the man was unfeasibly young and attractive for someone as unappealing as her, but she found their virtual interactions stimulating. She was thrilled to be asked out on a date, at her favourite Italian restaurant.

The man's name was Johnny Bird.

At the restaurant, he was charming, courteous and even more dishy in person, looking extremely dapper in his leather jacket and neatly trimmed goatee. He insisted from the outset on paying for everything, and during her second large glass of red wine, Lisa began to enjoy herself. Never mind the fifteen-year age gap, this was the best male attention she could remember having! He showed a huge interest in her job, what did she do, who did she work with, and sympathised hugely when she told him how difficult and stressful being a manager can be, especially when you have staff with personal problems. He asked what particular issues she had dealt with recently, and he listened reverently when she told him about her employee with the personal tragedy of a wife dying in childbirth, and the subsequent extreme problems with the child's physical abnormalities. The pressure of being a supportive manager was a heavy burden, and it was so cathartic to talk about this with someone who empathised and understood. Could Johnny finally be the soul mate she had craved for so many forlorn, lonesome years?

On a high, Lisa had arrived home after the date, eager to send Johnny a Facebook message and arrange another evening together. She was alarmed to find that there was no trace of Johnny's Facebook profile; it was not that he had simply de-friended Lisa, he had apparently removed all possible means of getting in touch. With a gut-wrenching sense of heartache and disappointment, she realised that despite her positive feelings about the date, clearly she was not in any way attractive to him, in fact to take the step of removing himself from Facebook altogether, he must have been utterly repulsed by her company. She howled and whimpered herself to sleep that night like an animal mourning the loss of its offspring to a predator.

Lisa took one final look at herself in the mirror and found herself nauseated by what she saw. A couple of days before, she had to make the heart-breaking decision to euthanize her elderly Yorkshire Terrier, who after months of careful nursing had finally lost her appetite as well as most of her sight and hearing. Lisa had lost her best friend and only regular companion. Someone up there obviously did not feel that she had enough strife and unhappiness in her life.

This was the final straw.

Catching her sobs, Lisa tottered unsteadily into the bathroom. The room was steamy from the hot bath she had run twenty minutes earlier. She put one foot in the water, flinching at the heat, and swung the other leg over. Sitting down ungracefully, she gave an involuntary yelp as the piping hot water swamped her sensitive parts, and water spilled all over the bathroom floor. She took several deep breaths, which were the only sounds apart from gentle sloshing of the water, and the droning whirr of the electric fan heater she held aloft.

"Goodbye, cruel world," said Lisa Plummer, and she plunged the heater into the cloudy water in front of her.

25

ABSOLUTE BEGINNER

Max thought the school was just the best thing ever! Miss Foster was very kind and pretty, even nicer than Julie. She was always asking him if everything was all right and did he have everything he needed?

He had enormous fun doing some painting, he had drawn a big picture of Matthew with big black spots and a big black nose. Miss Foster asked for a 'little' helper to wash up the painting things. The other children thought it was very funny when he was the first to put his hand up. She asked him not to get the cleaning cloth too dirty and he had a wonderful time seeing just how black and dirty he could get it. Rinsing the black powder paint directly into the cloth worked particularly well. He was in fits of giggles as he handed the filthy rag back to her.

And what a joy the music lesson was! All the class had a go on special toys called 'percussion instruments', Max's favourite was the cowbell, which didn't sound anything like a cow, but what a racket he could make with it! The children thought it was very funny when he bashed it against his crash helmet.

Max had got bored during something called 'assembly'.

All the children had to go into a big room and sit cross legged on the hard wooden floor. He had found it very uncomfortable trying to fold his legs and the nasty boy behind kept moaning that he couldn't see, and kept flicking Max's ears, which stuck out of the sides of his crash helmet. They had to sit quietly while Mrs Taylor made a boring speech and tried to teach them boring songs about someone called "Jesus" that just went on forever!

At lunchtime everyone liked his Brachiosaurus lunchbox and he got talking with the other boys about dinosaurs. Most boys liked Tyrannosaurus Rex the best, and one boy thought Pteranodon was BAD-ASS, but Max was happy with his Brackie.

The best fun of all was in a lesson called "Pee-Yee". They did running and jumping and climbing and Max could run faster, jump further and climb higher than anybody. Some of the other children kept saying "It's not fair!" and some cried. Miss Foster said that everyone is good at something and Max is good at Pee-Yee, other people will be better at things like reading and writing. But not painting or hitting the cowbell!

Max was very sad when the bell rang and it was time to go home. He gave Miss Foster a crushing bear hug and followed the other children to the outside door. Daddy and Julie were there to meet him, waving and then rushing up to collect him. He noticed the other mummies and daddies looking at him funny. One lady was staring at him. Daddy said it was rude to stare so Max stuck his tongue out at the lady. She was not very happy.

Matthew had obviously missed him while he was out, a couple of Daddy's books were shredded, strewn across the living room carpet as though they had exploded. Max got Daddy to show Matthew his painting. He sniffed it for a moment but then stood on his hind legs and gave Max a big hug. Julie stuck the painting to the front of the fridge.

After tea, Max was shattered, the excitement of the day had really got to him. Daddy said "Night night" and Julie kissed him on the cheek. Max said "I can't wait till tomorrow, Daddy. School is BRILLIANT!"

Unfortunately, Max and his Daddy would soon find that the feelings Max had toward the school were not reciprocated.

26

FLY HIGH

Max was staying with Bob and Bell that weekend. Mark felt it was important to ensure that his son was part of his grandparents' lives. Mark hoped that this weekend would be more successful than the previous time. Max had been taken to Alton Towers, and been prohibited from going on any rides because of his size. This was of course entirely foreseeable, a person nearing seven feet tall would be both uncomfortable and ridiculous in a children's roundabout or attempting to negotiate a helter skelter. And there would have been a serious risk of Max being decapitated on some of the more grown up rides – but he was too young for these anyway. It had been an unhappy experience for all of them and Mark had privately cursed Bob and Bell's common sense failure. Mark hated roller coasters and fairground attractions anyway; twenty years ago he had had a terrifying experience on the Alton Towers Corkscrew that had put him off such things for life.

This weekend, however, Bob and Bell were on safer ground: a trip to Twycross Zoo. This would be Max's first encounter with creatures larger than himself. He was very excited when Mark and Julie dropped him off at about ten o'clock Saturday morning.

It was a rare opportunity for Mark to have some quality time with Julie. They had been going out together for several months now, but in many ways were still getting to know each other. Julie was brilliant with Max and appeared not to be phased by his abnormality or the fate of his mother.

It was also a chance to unwind after a stressful week. Max had enjoyed his first few days at school and was apparently a hit with the other kids, much to Mark's surprise. Children would take it turns to have rides on Max's shoulders, in the playground naturally, and Max's bumping of his head and general gaucheness seemed to amuse his classmates. Max was also beginning to exhibit an impishness naughtiness as the incident with the cleaning cloth showed. However Mark, and to an extent Max also, were becoming conscious of whispers in the playground amongst the other parents. There was no doubt that Max's arrival at Southfields had caused a stir, and some people clearly had a difficulty with accepting people who are different. Mark made a mental note to speak with Mrs Taylor, perhaps she should write to parents to explain things to them. Not that clear explanations were easy to provide: Max was a boy who had grown too much, and was still growing. Not even Mark really understood why this was; neither Geoffrey Kelly or Doctor Crowe had provided convincing reasons, and Mark had not heard anything from either men recently.

It had also been an unsettling week at work. Lisa had not shown up all week, and had not called in sick. This was completely out of character. She had not answered her telephone or replied to emails and the office was full of wild theories about Lisa being kidnapped, or had been whisked away by a rich sugar daddy. Lisa's absence had left a management vacuum and even though she had been away for only a few days, routine decision making had ground to a halt; there was no nominated deputy for her. Head Office had been notified, but the Civil Service was slow to react at the best of times.

Mark and Julie drove into Leicester to have a mooch around the shops and a relaxing lunch. Julie had bought a new pair of jeans and some fetching black leather ankle boots. Mark had treated himself to some Vans trainers and a few science fiction DVDs. They ate at a moderately expensive but delicious Thai restaurant.

Julie, her long light brown hair tied back into a pony tail, looked particularly gorgeous today, Mark thought. Slender and attractive, she wore no make-up or jewellery, easily able to rely on her natural looks. Julie had told him a few stories from her younger years: Julie had been a county-standard swimmer at around the age of ten and eleven, although she had given this up by the time she left school. With a couple of girlfriends she got lost in Hampton Court maze, and had met the Spice Girls thanks to a TV phone-in competition (Sporty was the nicest, Posh the prettiest, Ginger the loudest). She had spent her gap year travelling but most of this time was spent in India, in which Julie had been spellbound by the people, the sights, sounds and aromas of a vibrant, diverse country. Her favourite colour was green. Julie shared this information in a self-effacing, light-hearted style, punctuated by an infectious giggle. At one stage, Mark became distracted as in his mind's eye a naked Julie, lying on her back and holding her legs in the air, urged him to do whatever he wanted to her. Mark couldn't get home soon enough.

When they did arrive home in mid-afternoon, Julie frisky after a few glasses of wine, Mark's fantasy, and one or two others, became a glorious reality.

27

POWER IN THE AIR

When Mark arrived at Southfields school on Monday afternoon to collect Max, the headteacher was waiting at the main entrance. She was talking intently with a short man of around sixty, Mark guessed, a full head of silvery hair with matching beard. He was dressed in a smart charcoal grey suit, and carried a briefcase.

Max had not yet emerged. Probably having too much fun aggravating Miss Foster, Mark speculated to himself. "Ah, Mrs Taylor, glad to catch you. Any chance I could have a quick word with you? I feel there's something we need to chat about."

"Good afternoon, Mr Anderson. Actually, there's something we wanted to discuss with you. This is George Cook, our Chairman of Governors." He nodded a silent hello.

"Oh, I see. If this is about Max being a bit naughty, I'm sure that between us we can address it."

"No Mr Anderson, it's not about Maxwell's....behaviour. Please come to my office, and we can have a proper conversation."

"But I need to wait here, for Max."

"Your son is quite happy and being well looked after by our staff. We'll talk in my office."

As Mark was led down the corridor, he felt as though it was he who was the naughty schoolboy, being led to the head's office for a telling off, detention, suspension or worse. Neither Mrs Taylor or George Cook spoke during the short walk, creating an awkward tension.

When they sat down at the meeting table, the Chairman next to the headteacher directly opposite him, Mark stayed silent and waited for one of them to explain what this was all about.

"Mr Anderson," began the headteacher, "as you know, here at Southfields we pride ourselves on diversity and equality in all matters. We embrace a culture of acceptance, and celebration of uniqueness and individuality."

"Individuality," affirmed Cook, unnecessarily.

Mrs Taylor continued, "We welcomed young Maxwell into our school, confident that as well as helping him to develop, he would make a valuable contribution to the life of our school."

"School," repeated Cook.

"However," said the Headteacher, "I have to balance the needs of the individual against the greater good of the school community as a whole. Are you a fan of Star Trek, Mr Anderson?"

Mark was thrown by this apparent non-sequitur. "Pardon?"

"Are you a fan of Star Trek, Mr Anderson?" she repeated, unblinkingly.

Mark, a huge fan of science fiction generally and Star Trek in particular, said, "Well, yes, I like it lot. I have most of the DVDs."

"Then you will be familiar with the aphorism 'The needs of the many outweigh the needs of the few'?"

"Yes, '...the needs of the few...or the one.' It's a central theme in the early Trek movies. Used to debate it all the time with an old schoolmate of mine."

"And do you accept the logic of this statement?"

Mark paused, wondering what this was leading up to. "It depends. Don't know, really. I suppose so. What's all this about?"

Mrs Taylor glanced at her Chairman, as if looking for permission to proceed; he gave an imperceptible silent nod.

She looked Mark in the eye and said firmly, "I'm afraid to have to say that the school has received some complaints about your son. From other parents, and some school staff. These are not about Maxwell's behaviour, he's no worse than any other boy. It's his – condition. We have had several people express the view that it is simply – unnatural. Some parents have threatened to take their children out of the school."

Mark, stunned, kept enough of his wits about him to realise that getting angry would not help him or his son in this situation. "What do you mean, 'unnatural'?"

"Mr Anderson, your infant son is nearly seven feet tall!"

"Tall!" said George Cook. Mark resisted the temptation to lean across the table and garrotte the Chairman with his own tie.

The headteacher said, "It's an inescapable fact that although popular with his classmates, your son's appearance is starting to have a destabilising effect on the school. It's only been a few weeks but the early signs are there. In the circumstances I've had no alternative but to take proactive action and discuss the matter with the Chairman of Governors and the Local Education Authority.

It's with much regret, Mr Anderson, that I must inform you that young Maxwell is no longer welcome at Southfields." She looked down at the table, suddenly a little bashful, self-conscious.

Mark spluttered, "That's disgraceful! You should tell those other parents to go to Hell! There's nothing wrong with my son. What am I supposed to do with him? He has the right to an education, just like anyone else!"

"I'm sorry, Mr Anderson, the decision has been taken. Maxwell will have to be educated at home."

"Home," chimed Cook. What an irritating twat, thought Mark.

"I can't believe you've given up on my son just like that. Can't you see how unreasonable this is, and how hard it will be on Max? He loves it here! I'm going to fight this to the very top!"

Neither the headteacher or Chairman had anything further to say. Mark went to collect his son. Max and Miss Foster emerged from a side room. Max came scampering toward him, brandishing a large piece of paper. "Look, Daddy! I painted a neff-el-ump and a zee-bra! Just like in the zoo!"

"That's great, Max, really good," said Mark and held Max's hand firmly as they walked out of the school, one figure towering over the other. Max banged his head on the doorframe for the last time.

28

WASTED LIFE

It had been the Thursday following Max's ejection from Southfields School. Mark was late for work, due to heavy traffic between his house and that of his parents. Roger and Shirley were looking after Max and Matthew that day. Mark had spent much of the previous two days bombarding the Local Education Authority with complaints of Max's treatment and demands for restitution. The LEA's Director of Education herself had eventually spoken to Mark and affirmed that the decision had been taken correctly and was irreversible. None of the County's other schools were judged to be equipped to manage Maxwell's condition, she had said. The LEA's focus would now be on supporting Mark with a programme of home tuition. Incensed, Mark had fired off angry emails to his County Councillor, the local MP, Secretary of State for Education and Prime Minister's Office. He filed a formal complaint with OFSTED and the Local Government Ombudsman. This activity would ultimately prove to be fruitless. Meanwhile, with bitter reluctance Mark made the necessary arrangements for Max to be educated at home.

When Mark arrived at the office that Thursday morning, the staff had been gathered for a meeting with the Regional

Manager, Craig Harding. Mark slid discreetly into the back of the group. He noticed Julie in the middle of the group, eyes moist as were those of several other colleagues. One of his younger male colleagues was sobbing. Mark frowned in disgust; Roger had brought him up with the doctrine "big boys don't cry".

Mark began to pick up Craig Harding's speech. He was a few years younger than Mark, immaculately dressed in designer suit, short spiky gelled hair. "....her cause of death will be reported in the local press this evening, so I'll reveal this to you now – Lisa died by electrocution, caused by an electrical appliance being introduced to the bath she was sitting in. There'll be an inquest of course, but I can say that the police are not looking for anyone else, and the circumstances would appear to indicate that, tragically, Lisa's death was due to suicide. I would point out though that no note was found so this is speculation until the inquest proceedings are concluded." The manager was an accomplished performer, conveying gravitas, compassion, sincerity and professional detachment in just the right proportions. He continued, "Lisa's funeral will be held next Thursday, two pm, at Melton Crematorium. The family have requested no flowers, with donations to Yorkshire Terrier Breed Rescue. Apparently Lisa was a dog lover. The office shall be closing on the day, so that everyone will be able to attend. Of course, this isn't compulsory."

Mark thought back to Lisa making a pass at him. Did his refusal contribute to her suicide? He was nice about it, wasn't he? He felt nauseous as icy pangs of guilt stabbed at his insides.

"What about Lisa's position, Mr Harding? Is it

going to be filled?" asked one of the supervisors, a little insensitively.

"The post is being re-evaluated, and if it's decided that recruitment is necessary, the post will be advertised shortly. Interim arrangements will be advised tomorrow. Meanwhile, anyone who feels it necessary can take today off."

Harding then called for a minute's silence, which was reverently observed; during this Mark realised that Lisa Plummer's funeral was to be held at the same crematorium that Michelle's had been held almost five years previously. The memories of Michelle's death and its aftermath were no longer quite as vivid, but the feelings of shock, sadness and injustice would still regularly rise to the surface. Mark had never received a satisfactory explanation of his wife's brutal emasculation. Lisa's funeral would inevitably reopen this wound.

Ashen, Mark went over to Julie, who was still fighting back tears. "Oh my God, Mark!"

"I'm devastated – it's just unbelievable. That poor woman. I had no idea she was so unhappy."

"Nor did I. Poor Lisa, what on Earth was she going through?"

"I'm afraid I might be partly responsible," said Mark as Julie's eyes widened. "Can I tell you something, in confidence?"

"You know you can trust me, Mark."

"I think it might be me that pushed Lisa over the edge. A few months ago she made a pass at me. I turned her down."

"Oh my God, Mark!" repeated Julie.

"I was shocked at the time, but I tried to be nice – let her down gently."

"That can't have been the only thing though. You don't kill yourself because of one brush off. There must have been other problems in her life. I guess none of us made the effort to get to know her well enough to have an idea what was going on."

"It's difficult when someone's the boss, though." Mark sighed. "You want to get out of here?"

Julie smiled. "I could use a cuddle right now."

29

THE SPIRIT AND THE FLESH

Mark and Julie arrived home, wired at the emotional strain of Lisa's suicide, and Max's expulsion from the school. He slumped down onto the sofa and cradled his head into his hands.

"That poor woman. My poor boy," he lamented and looked up at Julie, his face contorted with the strain of keeping his emotions under control. Wordlessly, she sat next time to him and put a supportive hand on his knee.

"It's all right, Mark, let it out. I'm here for you," she soothed. Unable to suppress his feelings any further, he enveloped her in his arms and hugged tightly, a gesture which she fully reciprocated. He let loose a primeval sob, and collapsed into her enveloping warmth in floods of tears. He felt helpless and exposed and yet, despite the conditioning of his childhood, it suddenly felt completely natural to unburden his feelings on Julie in this way. As his noisy weeping intensified, he realised that she had coaxed as complete an expression of his inner feelings from him as he had ever been able to give; even Michelle had not seen anything like this. His connection with Julie at this moment was unshakeably strong, he felt dependent, blissfully affectionate, and unprecedentedly intimate. In spite of himself, a part of his body started its own physical response, rapidly reaching an intensity to match the emotional electricity flowing between them.

Mark's feelings of shame at his raw show of emotion soon gave way to a frisson of embarrassment as Julie caressed the stiffening bulge of his jeans. He became conscious of Julie's quickening breath.

"Undress me," she commanded, thrillingly.

Usually a selfless, attentive lover, he felt a hot flush of guilty excitement as he pushed Julie's malleable form back on to the sofa, his own need for a sexual release overriding his every thought process. She emitted a surprised yelp, and smiled at him, at once bemused and self-conscious, yet wordlessly conveying to Mark an encouragement to go further. A warm, moist longing radiated across her groin. His cheeks flushed red with desire.

He hurriedly unbelted and unzipped, pulling down his jeans and briefs in one fluid movement. Julie quickly discarded her t-shirt. She neither wore nor needed a bra. Mark hooked his thumbs into her elasticated pedal-pushers and pulled them down to her ankles. She kicked them off, urgently, and he revelled in the wondrous sight of her nakedness.

Their coupling was vigorous, rapid and for Mark, blissfully explosive and shattering. He collapsed into her arms, spent and breathless, and sobbed as passionately as he had only a few minutes before. This time, they were tears of joy. She cuddled him, tenderly, until his composure returned.

"My turn," she whispered, husky and mischievous, and

pushed his eager head down to her warm, salty moistness below. His willingness to please her was as tireless as it was effective, fireworks went off in her head, and she had the absolute time of her life.

30

WHATEVER DAYS

The next few weeks were particularly busy.

Matthew broke a toe on one of his back paws, sustained by clipping the French window frame when belting into the house from the back garden. The end of the toe had to be amputated. Thankfully, the pet insurance company paid the substantial vet's bill.

Max's fifth birthday was celebrated with a cinema trip to see a new animated movie featuring, inevitably, friendly dinosaurs, somewhat incongruously living in the same world and timespan as humans. Max loved it, but Mark found the plot unfathomable, the scientific and historical anomalies irritating and the visuals too frenetic and bewildering; he was also uncomfortably embarrassed that the people sat behind his son kept muttering about not being able to see properly. Several times he turned around to whisper "sorry", to be met by hostile glares.

Afterwards, there was a family gathering at Roger and Shirley's house. Max's presents included an easel and painting set, and a book on how to draw animals. He had done little else since the zoo trip, much to Bob and Bell's delight. For the first time, no birthday wishes were received from Geoffrey Kelly, which troubled Mark.

Max was seven feet two inches tall on his birthday. Getting clothes and shoes was now becoming a serious operation, and expensive. No town centre or high street shop supplied items for people that big. Mark had found an American business on the internet that custom made clothes for outsized people, Four X Fashions. They specialised in massively obese people – the kind you see on TV shockumentaries being hoisted in and out of bed – but they were able to accommodate Max's requirements, at a price, naturally.

The home tuition programme began. Funded by the LEA, a tutor visited twice a week to go through some material, bring back marked homework, and set exercises to be done before next time. The tutor was Christine Sullivan, a frumpy woman of around fifty, short curly hair and thick glasses, and she wore aged Marks and Spencer outfits. She was kindly, patient and apparently a very competent teacher who took no nonsense while taking care to give praise for work well done. Mark liked her, and more importantly, Max seemed to also. Most sessions and homework were structured around an animal theme – spelling, grammar, even mathematics – which held Max's interest, and he learned quickly.

Head Office decided that Lisa's post should be filled. With strong encouragement from Julie, Mark applied for the post and was interviewed by a rather frosty panel of three senior civil servants, supported by a personnel officer, no doubt there to ensure due process was followed, and compliance with diversity and equality policies. Mark did not have time to prepare thoroughly for the interview and underperformed. The job was given to his colleague Dinesh Parmar, and Mark was quietly relieved. On reflection, he did not need the pressure that taking on more responsibility would entail.

Mark's sister Marie got engaged to an older woman she had met on a recent Mediterranean cruise. Marie's sexuality had never been openly discussed in the family, but Mark was not at all surprised, even if his parents seemed shocked. He sent Marie a card and note expressing his good wishes. No wedding date had been set.

So, there was plenty going on in Mark's life. On the first Sunday in December, Mark and Julie, in bed and tightly nuzzled together, were woken up when the phone rang at about eight a.m. It was his friend, Freddie Abbott. "Jesus Christ, Marky, you seen the paper this morning?" Mark replied that he had not, in fact he was still in bed with his gorgeous girlfriend, thank you very much.

"Well, get your pants on and check out the Mail website."

Mark jumped out of bed, leaving Julie to her semi-conscious murmuring. He looked in on Max – playing happily with Brackie and a large cuddly elephant, a birthday gift from Julie. Matthew was curled up happily on Max's bed, licking his damaged paw.

He switched on his PC and waited the maddening couple of minutes it took to boot up and enable the broadband connection. He Googled the Mail on Sunday and went straight to their website.

The lead headline hit Mark like a punch from a heavyweight boxer.

31

LANDSLIDE

EXPELLED:
'FREAK' BOY BANNED FROM COUNTY'S SCHOOLS
Exclusive by Mail reporter, Johnny Bird

Education chiefs in Leicestershire were being praised last night by parents who had successfully campaigned for a pupil attending their local primary school to be excluded.

The five year old boy, named locally as Maxwell Anderson, has a unique genetic growth deformity which has caused him to reach seven feet in height by the time of his fifth birthday. He had been attending Southfields primary school in Melton Mowbray, Leicestershire until angry mums voiced their concerns.

Local parent Mrs Kayleigh Robins, 27, told the Mail: "Many of the mums and dads at Southfields feel it is both ridiculous and dangerous for a seven foot tall boy to be at the school. The risk to other children is just too great."

"That boy is a freak," said another mum, who did

not wish to be named. "It's not natural. Whatever he's got could spread to my kids. They should never have let him come to the school in the first place."

And single father Mr Joseph Brett, 24, said: "I feel sorry for Max and his Mum and Dad, but the lad is just enormous – it's quite unbelievable. I wasn't happy for my lad to be in the same class."

Neither the Headteacher, Mrs Diana Taylor, or the Chairman of Governors, Mr George Cook, were available for comment last night. A spokesman for the County Council said, "The Local Education Authority is proud of its culture of embracing diversity and equality. However, after a careful review of this case it was concluded for health and safety reasons that there were no facilities in the County's schools that would adequately cater for Maxwell Anderson's condition. We are working closely with the boy's family to ensure that a comprehensive programme of home tuition is delivered."

Sources close to the local maternity hospital where Maxwell was born have told the Mail that they do not know what has caused the abnormal growth, or what height the boy may reach when fully grown. Said one insider: "This is a truly unique case, and presents a significant opportunity for research."

The Guinness Book of Records was understood to be closely monitoring the Maxwell case. The tallest recorded human being, Robert Wadlow, who died in 1940 aged 22, reached 8 feet 11 inches in height.

The Mail has obtained an exclusive photograph of Maxwell Anderson and his father. It shows an otherwise normal boy, towering over his father and happily holding his hand as they walk to school.

More photographs and exclusives on the Maxwell Anderson story will appear in the Mail during the next few weeks.

Do YOU think education chiefs were right to ban Maxwell Anderson? Text MAX YES or MAX NO to 89099. Texts cost 15 pence + normal message rate. Ask bill payer's permission.

32

CALIFORNIA NIGHTS

Johnny Bird was ecstatic. His first front page story, this was the finest achievement in his career so far. His editor was reluctant to run the story at first, at least not quite as prominently, but Johnny had great powers of persuasion. Just ask the young blonde who came home with him last night, pulled from the Birmingham nightclub Johnny went to after the presses began rolling. She was still dozing in Johnny's bed. He struggled to recall her name.

Johnny was ambitious, but mainly with the objective of boosting his personal profile, so he could get more girls. After spells working with the local free newspaper and the BBC radio station, two years ago he had got his big break as an intern at the Mail. He had worked his way up from the classified adverts to the sports desk and eventually the news desk. He became prominent in the editor's thoughts after he had scooped the story of this year's best male singer Brit Award being caught getting sucked off by the best female newcomer at the backstage party.

He looked at himself in the mirror; running his hands through his tousled hair, and stroked his neatly trimmed goatee beard. "You're going places, my son," he told his reflection.

He re-read the article. It was pretty much as he'd delivered it, although the sub had trimmed a little of the wording here and there. The picture was a little grainy, and the art department had unnecessarily pixelated the faces of Maxwell and his father. As if that would stop them being identified!

"Johnny! I'm thirsty and horny. Bring me a drink and let's fuck!" called the girl from the bedroom.

"In a minute, babe." He reached for a manila folder which that odious man Kelly had given him. Flicking through, he pondered which of the documents to use in his next story. Papers on gigantism research? DNA test results? The mother's autopsy report?

Johnny pulled out one sheet in particular and smiled to himself. This is the one. A grainy photo of the six month scan from inside the womb. There was young Maxwell, tiny, fragile. A larger figure was nestled against him.

Johnny Bird grinned triumphantly, eagerly anticipating the day he would reveal to the world that Maxwell Anderson had a twin brother.

33

MERCY STREET

This being a Sunday, naturally Mark could not get hold of anyone at the school. Geoffrey Kelly was not answering any of the numbers Mark had for him. The maternity hospital stonewalled him, no-one in authority was available to discuss the article. Mark demanded to know who the "sources" and "insider" were, but the people he spoke to were either unwilling or unable to assist.

Julie was there, of course, and within an hour of phoning, Roger and Shirley arrived to provide moral support and look after Max and Matthew while Mark attempted to deal with this new crisis. They had had to run the gauntlet of a phalanx of press photographers. Mark wondered how they had got his address. Electoral roll, presumably.

What he really wanted to do was get hold of the reporter, Johnny Bird, and wring his bloody neck. And the Mail's editor, too. How dare they invade his family's privacy? How dare they label his son a 'freak'? And what did they mean, that more photographs and exclusives would appear? How were they getting this information? And who from? The school, the hospital, the office? His family? Surely not.

So many questions. Roger entered the room and gave a

supportive, paternal smile. "The womenfolk are busy with Max. Shirley will sort some food out shortly."

Mark grunted acknowledgement. "What should I do, Dad?"

"If it was me, son, I'd get a solicitor onto the paper, pronto. Sue them for plenty. Let them know they can't bully someone just because he stands out from the crowd." No pun was intended by Roger, he had little concept of irony.

"But there's nothing factually incorrect in the article. And the 'freak' comments are attributed to local people, it's not the paper saying that."

"Wouldn't hurt to lay a marker down, would it? And you could get a 'cease and desist' order slapped on 'em."

Mark was reaching for the Yellow Pages when the phone rang again.

"May I speak with Mr Anderson, please?" a voice said, in a plummy, aristocratic tone.

"That's me. Who is this?"

"My name is Ralph Perkins. I would like to offer my services."

"And what services would these be, Mr Perkins?"

"Please, call me Ralph. And may I call you Mark? I'm the owner and director of Ralph Perkins Public Relations, RPPR, perhaps you've heard of us? I'm a public relations consultant – I help people who unexpectedly find themselves in the media eye. I can turn this drama into an opportunity. You'll look back on today as the start of something wonderful."

Something wonderful, now where have I heard that before, thought Mark.

"Mr Perkins – er, Ralph, I'm not sure that's what I need right now. I was just trying to get hold of a solicitor."

"You just leave that loathsome twerp Johnny Bird to me. And the Mail – squalid little rag, should have known better. Let me make some calls and I'll be with you by lunchtime."

"Well, I don't know..."

"See you shortly, Mark. Don't answer the phone again till I see you, which will be very soon. Don't worry! Cheerio!"

Mark's head was spinning. What the hell was he getting into?

34

THE DOOR

Ralph Perkins replaced the telephone receiver and congratulated himself on a productive morning's work. This is the break I'm looking for, he thought.

The Ralph Perkins Public Relations empire consisted of a small office, converted from the third bedroom in his reasonably sized semi-detached house, located in one of the least unattractive estates on the outskirts of Coventry.

This was the latest in a long line of business ventures for Ralph. Now aged about sixty, his first job upon leaving a Birmingham middle school in the early seventies was a greengrocer's assistant in the local corner shop, in an era when such establishments were still prevalent and prosperous. Keen to spread his wings, in his late teens Ralph took a job as a lighthouse keeper's mate, involving month long spells spent in isolation in lighthouses off the Cornish shoreline, with just his senior officer for company. Talk about growing up fast! Eventually the seclusion – and the noisy, windy nights got too much for Ralph. The final straw was a dream he had about descending the spiral stone staircase, and never reaching the bottom. Back in Birmingham, he spent an unhappy year labouring on building sites before deciding he should make something of himself. His first attempt was running a car washing and valeting business, beginning with a sponge and bucket and eventually establishing a drive through site and an enterprise big enough to employ six people. Subsequently, Ralph had tried his hand at being a wine salesman, running a market stall selling sports equipment (cricket was a passion of his), a recruitment consultant, rock band manager and private investigator. Shortly after turning fifty, Ralph took inspiration from the example of Max Clifford, PR guru to the stars, with flashy car and enormous house. Ralph wanted a piece of that action!

Unfortunately, Ralph had not quite found the big time. Amongst his clients so far had been a Premiership footballer convicted for drunk driving, a local authority which owned a swimming pool where, tragically, a young girl had got into difficulties and drowned, and an MP with embarrassing questions asked about her expenses. All of these people needed a more positive media profile. Ralph had helped most of them achieve this, but it was hardly the glitzy rubbing shoulders with celebrities he had assumed would come his way.

Until now, perhaps. Ralph routinely scanned the major news outlets, looking for signs of someone in trouble, someone who would need his particular brand of 'help'. When he saw the Mail's lead story, a bright neon white light bulb exploded in his head. He could immediately see the opportunities for the Anderson family – and himself. After all, his standard terms were a twenty-five per cent cut, expenses on top. Ralph made one more phone call, finessed his appearance, and started the drive to Melton Mowbray, a buzz of anticipation coursing through his veins.

Yes, today was going to be his day.

35

CLOUDBURST

His gaze darted across the screen like a hyperactive wasp, his pink eyes sparkling with an intense, insatiable curiosity. His blood surged as a swell of raw, primal excitement arose in the pit of his stomach, igniting a fuse of intensity that burnt through his entire body. He felt like sparks of static electricity were exploding from his skin. A throbbing erection strained against his black leather trousers – but this was not sexual arousal. It was the thrill of realising that finally, the cause he was destined to champion had finally revealed itself.

Devouring the internet coverage, starting with the Mail Online site, he shunned the celebrity gossip clickbait and scooped up as many different versions of the Maxwell Anderson story from other sites as he could find, his fingers on the trackpad ablur. Comments were spreading across social media like a supersonic tsunami, and he 'liked', 'favourited' and 'followed' all the comments and posters he encountered. As he well knew, a proportion of these would follow him back. His band of Followers had been dwindling lately, impatient for action after five years of broken promises and abandoned struggles. Time to replenish!

The wonderment he was feeling crumbled and gave way to awe, reverence and a purifying clarity. Maxwell Anderson is The Chosen One. Here, at last, was the fated mission to lead his Followers on a golden crusade of positive action.

The opportunity to make an indelible and glorious mark on history.

36

AINT SEEN NOTHING LIKE ME

By the end of the day, Ralph had negotiated a substantial payment from the Mail in response to an exclusive serialisation of the Maxwell Anderson story. In addition, an in-principle agreement with the Channel 4 Dispatches programme had been reached to make a film about Max. Ralph had also put feelers out to some major toy companies, angling for some sort of product endorsement deal.

This had taken several hours of hard discussion with Mark, together with Julie, Roger and Shirley, all of whom Mark wanted to be involved. The advantages of engaging RPPR to represent them, and to seek publicity and commercial deals of the type Ralph had in mind, included the promise that they could control the agenda, rather than have surprise revelations sprung upon them. The potential financial rewards were also persuasive; Mark was starting to seriously struggle with the sheer cost of feeding and clothing his still-growing son; a specially-made reinforced bed had recently set him back five thousand pounds, not including the cost of custom-sized bedding, helpfully supplied by Four X Fashions.

Shirley was the most vocal opponent of Ralph's

proposals. She could not accept that there was moral justification for exploiting her grandson in this way.

"I understand, Mrs Anderson," Ralph had soothed, in that upper crust accent of his, "but this money could be used to ensure that your son and grandson are financially secure for life. Apart from anything else, the money could be used to ensure that the best possible education is obtained for young Max. And there is the question of healthcare."

Mark's attention snapped into focus. "Ralph, what do you mean?"

"I hesitate to do this, folks, but let's be realistic about the quality of life young Max can expect as his, er – condition – develops. Right now, he's a happy young boy, and that's great! Surely, though, we can expect his sheer bulk to put serious pressure on his young body, especially his bones and organs. You've told me, Mark, that the lad already sometimes has the kinds of aches and pains you don't tend to get until you're, well, my sort of age. As time goes on, you can anticipate serious back trouble, bone problems...disorders of the circulatory system, to say nothing of the psychological issues. Max will need a lot of counselling. Face facts, folks, as Max gets older, he'll require growing amounts of specialist care. Don't expect to get this on the NHS! We're talking expensive private clinics, probably abroad. Health insurance will be out of the question, too. I'm sorry to lay this on with a trowel, but there is a harsh financial reality to Max's abnormality, and you simply MUST make provision for it."

Ralph exhaled audibly, puffing his cheeks out. The group sat in awestruck silence, taken aback by the harshness of Ralph's words, but each of them accepting the truth of them. Long, difficult years lay ahead.

Roger broke the silence. "You're a bit quiet, Julie. What do you think?"

"I – I don't know. It's not for me to say." Julie shifted uneasily in her seat and looked witheringly at Mark. She's not happy, he thought. But he knew what had to be done. He stood, and four pairs of eyes regarded him expectantly.

"I'm Max's father, and your help and contributions are fantastic, but at the end of the day it's me who's responsible for keeping him safe. We're in an unbelievable situation. No-one's ever had to face anything like this before. I have to do everything within my power to give Max the best life I can. Ralph's right, we need to get real. I know that taking money from big business is risky, but sometimes life is about juggling risks and choosing between lesser evils. We're already strugging, to be honest, and it's going to get harder. Max is going to need care, and the media will be coming for us with or without the financial help. We need the money, and we need Ralph's help."

"But, Mark, you can't possibly..." cut in Shirley.

"Mother, it's not up to you. I'm doing this. We're doing this."

"None of you will regret this, Mrs Anderson," said Ralph. "Trust me, I'll look after them both." There was no further argument. Mark shook hands with Ralph and he activated his cellphone, and got straight to work.

Mark went upstairs to see his son. Toys were strewn around the room, including the innards of a cuddly toy giraffe, a victim of Matthew's. Max was curled up asleep, arms around the Dalmatian. Mark felt a surge of love towards his son. "I'm trying to do the best for you, young man," he whispered. In unison, Max and Matthew let out quiet purring snores.

Outside, the photographer pack started to slink away, called off by their editors. News of the exclusive deal was already spreading.

37

ROAD DOG BLUES

Johnny Bird was furious. How dare they interfere? He had carefully planned a sequence of exposés, each with new revelations, culminating in a sensational piece about the missing twin brother. Some of the material he had bought from Geoffrey Kelly was absolute dynamite.

This barrage of stories would mean that he would be the in-demand reporter of his generation. He would always be in high paid work. Not only that, possible book deals and maybe even a film adaptation, all based on his research, his legwork. He even had the title, "The Tall Tale of Maxwell Anderson." He would be rich beyond the dreams of avarice, and have all the girls he could cope with – and he reckoned he could cope with a lot.

But now the arsehole editor at the Mail had told him in no uncertain terms to drop the story. A deal had been struck with the family to serialise the story, which was expected to sell at least a quarter of a million extra copies on the days it appeared in the paper. There was high expectation that many people would start buying the Mail permanently, switching from the competitor publications. However, the family's representative had insisted on one important condition.

No Johnny Bird.

The family were aggrieved by the privacy invasion without their foreknowledge or permission. The angle taken by Bird had caused undue distress and unusually large payments for the story rights had been required in order to ward off a substantial damages claim. They had been especially upset that the boy's name and school had been named without prior warning. Now that the story was out the family had little choice but to engage with the media but they had insisted that they would control the agenda and work in partnership with the Mail. Any possible relationship the family could have forged with Johnny had foundered before it started.

So the editor bumped Johnny off the story and to add insult to injury moved him from the news features desk onto the home and garden weekend supplement. He was to surrender to the editor all materials in his possession regarding the Anderson story. He must not put out any material on the Maxwell Anderson story through any other publications or by social media, or, the editor said, he would personally see to it that Johnny would never work again. His new assignment was to critique the relative effectiveness of solar panels and cavity wall insulation in relation to reducing energy bills. What a waste of his great talent, Johnny thought, and as importantly, think of how many girls such an unglamorous job would make him miss out on.

This was NOT acceptable.

It did not take Johnny long to make his mind up. The course of action to take was obvious and clear. It would take some setting up, though, but he had the contacts, and what he lacked in patience, he made up for in determination, ingenuity and charm. With a smirk and a tingle of anticipation, and an adrenaline rush fuelled by snorting a line of coke, he reached for his phone.

38

A WHOLE NOTHER TRIP

Mark, Julie and Max were in the living room waiting for the camera crew to complete the painstaking process of setting up and aligning the equipment and lighting correctly. The crew of three, two men and a female producer who was in charge, had been there a couple of hours already. The producer, Hayley, twenty-something, short and petite with close cropped black hair and snazzy designer glasses, would also be asking the questions from behind the camera, for the family to deliver replies to as part of the documentary being filmed for Channel 4. Matthew found the whole process fascinating, and insisted on sniffing each new piece of kit as it was produced, not to mention requiring frequent cuddles from the three crew members. As cute and adorable as Matthew was, Hayley was starting to get a little harassed. She checked her watch frequently in increasingly exaggerated gestures.

Ralph was there, of course. He had been an almost permanent fixture in the month or so since the contracts were signed. He graciously left the family to itself for a few days either side of Christmas, but otherwise they had seen him every day in order to respond to the latest media interest, and to develop plans for upcoming events. Today he was looking at his protégés with fatherly pride; they had been model clients so far. Receptive to guidance and confident performers, and above lucrative fee earners. Ralph took a moment to sniff his pink carnation, resplendently tucked into his buttonhole, and patiently awaited the crew to complete its work.

Julie was playing Lego with Max, improvising oddly shaped and coloured spaceships. Max, now five and a quarter, had reached seven feet five inches tall. He was growing at the steady rate of about an inch a month. He was splayed awkwardly, the floor a sea of oversized limbs.

Mark was thinking about the path down which he had taken the people he loved. Dinesh, his new boss, had graciously approved an extended and indefinite (unpaid) leave of absence for Julie and himself. Their jobs would be held open for them, when they were ready to return. Meanwhile, Dinesh appeared to appreciate the exceptional circumstances involved, and supported Mark's request to take time out to get on top of the media issue and ensure his family and Max in particular were receiving the support they needed. However, Mark did have some uneasy thoughts about the appearances in the media they were now cultivating, in print, online and now, today, preparing to participate in a mass market television event. The original Johnny Bird piece had undoubtedly opened Pandora's Box and Mark accepted that Max would stay in the public eye whether they had liked it or not. Either they would be done unto by the media, or they would have to drive the agenda. It was the correct decision to sign up with Ralph and use his expertise to manage this process. The money flowing in was undoubtedly easing Mark's financial worries, and now that Max was out of school, there were reduced risks of continuing to expose him to the outside world. But Mark was conscious that Max would always be a public figure and notwithstanding the extreme growth, would never have a life that resembled what most people would regard as normal.

Julie had been brilliant throughout, and Mark was madly in love with her. She was sexy and, Mark mused wistfully, she was deliciously rude in the bedroom (and occasionally, elsewhere). She was a good listener, patiently allowing Mark to sound off when he needed to, and she was a good judge of when to suggest solutions and when to just listen and be supportive. She adored Max, who apparently worshipped her.

His parents, Roger and Shirley, were sympathetic to what Mark was doing with Ralph, but did not want to be the subject of any publicity themselves. They had declined all requests to participate, and it was now a condition of Mark and Max's involvement that no approaches would be made to his parents. Mark had spoken to his mother a few times per week, but the family had not been together since Boxing Day, about a month ago.

Max's other grandparents, Bob and Bell, had disappeared off the radar in recent months. A Christmas card had been received, without any warm messages, but Max had not seen them since before his birthday at the end of October. This lack of contact troubled Mark when he thought about it, but there seemed little opportunity to address the situation, without risking involving them in the publicity which they presumably would wish to avoid, like Roger and Shirley.

"Mark, Julie, we're ready to start," said Hayley, flustered, as the cameraman and boom operator got into position and ran their final checks.

Mark took a deep breath and faced the camera. "I'm ready," he said.

39

LONG STORY

Hayley began by asking, "What does Max enjoy doing?"

"Well, in many ways, he's just like any other normal, healthy boy." As he had been instructed, Mark looked directly at Hayley, who was sitting just behind and to the right of the camera. "He loves playing with his toys – Lego is his current craze, but he also likes his toy jungle animals, you know the kind of thing."

"Don't forget Brackie!" interjected Julie.

"Oh yes, I forgot. Max simply adores the dinosaurs, especially Brackie, and it's obvious why! He's also a budding young artist, he was inspired by a trip to the zoo. So far his talent hasn't matched his enthusiasm, but hey, he's only five!"

"What about sports, or music?" prompted Hayley.

"This is where having to come away from school is hard for Max. In the brief time he spent at Southfields primary, he loved music lessons, and was boisterous in his use of the percussion instruments. He never really got to do outdoor sports but he had fun in the gymnasium, where his height gave him a huge advantage, and enabled him to do things which the other kids found hugely entertaining. These days

Max doesn't have access to the facilities or classmates to enjoy these activities." Mark glared angrily directly into the heart of the camera lens, his eyes emitting a glower of resentment towards Diana Taylor, George Cook and the policy wonks at the Local Education Authority.

"And how is Max at personal relationships? Does he have many friends?"

"Not really, not since leaving school, and of course we're worried about this. Apart from myself and Julie, his best friend is Christine, his personal tutor. And Brackie, probably."

Julie cut in again. "Aren't you going to mention Matthew?"

"Oh shit, I should have mentioned him first. Hayley, can we start again?"

"No, we keep rolling, we can sort this out in the editing suite." She paused. "Who's Matthew – an invisible friend?" She should know, thought Mark. She's been tripping over him all afternoon.

"Max is fondest of our Dalmatian, Matthew. He's a lovely old dog, coming up to nine years old. They're practically inseparable, they're always playing together, or cuddled up, sleeping together. They're very cute. Sorry can we stop for a minute?" Mark was getting a little dewy eyed, which he'd rather not be made obvious to a few million people when this goes out. Big boys don't cry.

After a short break, Hayley asked, "What are the practical difficulties Max faces in day to day life?"

"Well, we're at the point where living in an unadapted house like this is becoming unmanageable. Max does not fit under doors, he still wears a crash helmet. This is not good for self-confidence. Bathing and showering is difficult – and there's a large surface area to wash! We also find that going to the bathroom itself is logistically difficult. There's.....a lot of mess." Mark winced – realising how embarrassing this would be for his son when this segment was replayed to him in later life.

"Then there's the challenge of keeping him in clothes and shoes that fit. Everything is made specially and shipped in – at huge expense." Mark looked directly at the camera again, as he had been coached by Ralph. "Financial pressures are becoming a major worry. Is this OK?"

"You're doing fine Mark, we'll be intercutting this with footage of Max bumping his head, trying clothes on et cetera. Please go on."

"One of the issues is that despite his size, Max is still really just a five year old boy. People we meet assume that he must be some sort of retard – I find this particularly annoying. Christine reckons that Max is of slightly above average intelligence and aptitude for his age."

"Tell them about eating, Mark." This was Julie.

"No, you do that, he likes your cooking better than mine."

"He is ALWAYS hungry. I know you could say that of most young boys, but Max is insatiable. His calorie intake is about five thousand per day, and it still doesn't seem enough. All types of pizza and pasta, chips of course, and very fond of peanut butter sandwiches. The cost of the food is also an issue. He's a messy eater, so there's a lot of cleaning involved....to say nothing of the washing up!"

Hayley asked, "Mark, what do you feel the future holds for Max?"

"That's a good question, really good. I think about it

all the time. You would think he has to stop growing soon. Max will clearly never be able to lead a normal life, he will always attract attention to himself. At seven and a half feet tall, there's a risk of various musculoskeletal disorders and circulatory problems at a young age; Robert Wadlow died at twenty-two. But that's not what I worry about the most."

"And what would that be, Mark?"

"What if Max DOESN'T stop growing?"

40

WHEN THINGS SLOW DOWN

Johnny Bird, pissed off after a day writing about the various methods of killing slugs and other garden pests – drowning them in Tesco's Value Bitter seemed the most economical way – perched on an armchair and switched the plasma television on to Channel 4. The Dispatches programme was about to begin.

He was curious, nervous and excited. His fame and fortune were inextricably linked to the media's interest in the Maxwell Anderson story. He was incensed – it should have been HIM that brought this to the world!

The adverts and trailers finished and Johnny braced himself for the documentary. Infuriatingly, another advert began – the programme was "sponsored by" a price comparison website. And then the show began.

The bastards! They had even nicked his title, "The Tall Tale of Maxwell Anderson." He was cursing his negligence in failing to copyright it, just as he had failed to register the obvious domain names before the Anderson family had done so, or more likely, their media representatives.

He would have to get smarter, sharpen up. Need to be ruthless to succeed in this game. He snorted another line of coke, and savoured the rush.

He watched the half-hour programme intently. It was actually very well put together, he had to concede. Moving, without being schmaltzy. Fascinating, but not sensationalist. And by the end, he actually found himself growing fond of the boy, and sympathetic to the burden his father was trying to cope with.

And he especially liked the girlfriend, Julie. Blimey, she was fit. Johnny would have to get to know her better!

As the programme finished, credits rolling over film of Maxwell playing tug of war with his spotty dog, Johnny reached for his cell phone and dialled a number.

He did not bother with small talk. "Did you watch it? What did you think?"

A pause. "Aha. Well, is our arrangement still on? We still good to go?"

Another pause. "Yes, the money's all lined up. I'll meet you at the place we discussed. Next Tuesday, eight p.m.?"

When Johnny's interlocutor had finished speaking, Johnny said, "That's great, Bob, thanks a lot my friend. Oh, and give my regards to Bell, will you?"

Immediately after terminating the call, the whole room seemed to shake as he was jolted by a thunderous hammering on the outer door. A sick feeling of terror consumed him; the rush of the coke instantly neutralised. A booming, action movie voice filled the air.

"POLICE! OPEN UP!"

41

INSIDE HIS PRESENCE

The Leader closed his eyes, savouring the moment, trying to burn the television images of The Chosen One into his retinas.

He would later scrutinise every nuance, every frame and pixel; absorbing the essence of Maxwell Anderson. The details of His life. The reasons for His existence.

Gleaning material to inspire his growing army of Followers.

Energised, he set his subconscious mind to work on crafting exhortations, and began his second viewing of the programme.

42

FREAK

Robert Wadlow was born in in the small city of Alton, Illinois in 1918, the eldest of five children. At birth he was a normal size, his recorded birth weight of eight pounds and six ounces was by no means exceptional. His father, Harold, was reasonably tall, at just under six feet, but again this was not in any way extraordinary.

By the time he began attending elementary school, Robert was five feet four inches tall, about half as big again as the average five year old. A special desk had to be constructed for him.

Robert, at age thirteen the world's tallest Boy Scout, seven feet four inches, had averaged a growth of four inches per year since birth. By the time he graduated from college, having studied law, he was just over eight feet tall.

Robert became a celebrity, touring with the Ringling Brothers Circus, and made many personal appearances. The public marvelled at the height, and also the size of Robert's feet, which reached size 37AA. Robert became a Freemason at a young age, reaching the sublime degree level of Master Mason.

Robert continued to grow steadily. On June 27, 1940,

eighteen days before Robert's death, doctors at Washington University in St Louis measured him at eight feet, eleven point one inches.

Robert stubbornly refused to use a wheelchair, relying on leg braces to walk. Towards the end of his life, he had little feeling in his legs and feet. On July 4, 1940, during a professional appearance at the Manistee National Forest Festival, a faulty leg brace caused a blister on his ankle. This became infected, and despite a blood transfusion and emergency surgery, Robert died in his sleep eleven days later. At death, Robert weighed thirty-one stones and five pounds. He was twenty-two years old.

Robert's funeral four days later was attended by five thousand people. His coffin was ten feet long and weighed half a ton. It required twelve pallbearers to carry it. Robert's family were concerned that his body would be the target of ghoulish treasure seekers, so the coffin was interred in a vault of solid concrete.

Life-size statues of Robert were erected at his birthplace of Alton, and at the Guinness Museum in Niagara Falls. Several replica models exist in Ripley's Believe It or Not Museums. They are all eight feet eleven point one inches high.

Maxwell Anderson passed Robert Wadlow's height two months before his eighth birthday.

43

INTERLUDE

It had been Bob and Bell's betrayal that had hurt Mark the most. Johnny Bird's behaviour was understandable, almost forgivable. He was just a cheap hack desperate to make a quick buck and get himself noticed. Well, he had achieved that all right. With Bob and Bell's help, he had produced lurid semi-fictional stories that had been picked up by a couple of the tabloids even more down market than the Mail, along with some sensationalist websites. The three of them had collaborated on a poorly written book.

Bob and Bell, Max's maternal grandparents, apparently never got over their daughter's premature death. After Melanie's funeral, they never properly engaged with Mark or Max, and were spooked by Max's abnormality. In some of the articles, and the travesty of a book, they blamed Mark for what happened to Melanie. He had failed to secure appropriate ante natal care, they said. When Max was small as a baby, he should have waited for his son to grow naturally, or at the very least get a second or third opinion, before consenting to unorthodox, probably illegal treatment. They felt excluded from their grandson's life. Mark had banned them, probably under Julie's influence, they said. Julie had been totally livid.

After the first couple of articles, Mark had reached out to Bob and Bell in an attempt to reconcile any differences and avoid further unnecessary publicity. Calls and emails went unanswered, apart from a terse instruction to direct all correspondence to their legal representatives.

The immediate aftermath from the Channel 4 programme had included a deluge of generosity from companies and individuals alike. Some people had been sufficiently moved to make anonymous donations towards Max's escalating living costs. Letters had flooded in from all parts of the country, and from all ages. One anonymous benefactor had sent a cheque for a quarter of a million pounds; one young child had sent a pound coin sellotaped to a crude drawing of a Maxwell stick figure towering over a tree. Mark and Julie made a point of sending thank you letters to every identifiable donor.

Ralph was happy of course; such donations were channelled through his office, and he was on twenty-five per cent. A new Lexus in gold metallic finish was one of many extravagances funded from his commission.

Many unsolicited donations of goods were received, ranging from peanut butter and pizza to cleaning products and artists' materials. All of these came with endorsement deals which on Ralph's advice Mark was happy to sign. The companies concerned would do well having Max as their poster boy.

Four X Fashions, with whom Mark had invested increasingly startling amounts of cash in the futile process of keeping Max in clothes and shoes that fit, offered free supplies for as long as they could use Max in their international advertising. This generous move alone was to save Mark many thousands of pounds a year.

Through the corporate sponsorships and private donations, together with the income from media, Mark found himself in the comfortable position of being able to resign from his Civil Service position. Julie decided to continue in work; she was supportive of Mark but needed an ongoing grounding in reality. She was still maintaining her own house, although slept at Mark's at least three or four times a week.

With Ralph still on board, and despite the twenty-five per cent, providing invaluable assistance, Mark had managed to secure an affordable deal with a house builder to construct a custom made facility, capable of accommodating a person of Mark's stature. Doorways were built ten feet high, Max would have a bedroom suitably proportioned, even his own bathroom – at nearly nine feet tall, conventional utilities were fast becoming useless.

So, Mark reflected, the decision to engage with the media had helped his son's life more than it had harmed it. The family was financially comfortable; not quite secure for life, but money was not something to worry about for the time being. Max did not seem to have any memory of Bob and Bell, and certainly was not missing them. And now that he had broken the Wadlow record, and was the tallest human being ever known to have lived, surely he would stop growing soon!

Roger, ever the pragmatist, could always be relied on to keep Mark's feet on the ground. He had the uncanny knack of puncturing any rare displays of optimism that Mark allowed himself.

"Remember, son," Roger had said on one visit, "Money can buy many things but not the most important of all.

Health and happiness are priceless. Don't tempt fate and never let your guard down."

Wise words, indeed.

44

LIVING OUT LOUD

Max felt happy. What a fun day with Christine it had been! They had done reading, with his favourite Famous Five story about the gold smugglers, then they had done science, all about planets! He had learned about Jupiter and Saturn, and a spaceship called "Voyager", which was really a cool robot! Then a bit of maths, which he didn't really like, but was quite good at, so he was rewarded with an art session, and he painted a brilliant picture of a giraffe eating a tree. And finally, Christine had taught him some history, all about a famous king called Henry the Eighth, who chopped the heads off his wives! History was awesome!

Then, he watched a DVD of Road Runner cartoons, his favourite cartoon character, Wile E Coyote, was very funny. Max had laughed himself silly when he had put up the tiny umbrella to stop the anvil crashing down on his head.

Best of all, his tea had been yummy! Not one, two but THREE pizzas – all with his favourite toppings, pineapple, tuna, pepperoni and mushrooms. In fact, as he said to Daddy and Julie many times, it was scrumptious bumptious tiddly-um pumptious! It was nasty of Daddy, though, to tell him to shut up, but Matthew and Brackie were very chuffed, and they didn't mind how many times they were told.

They were his BEST friends!

45

TRANSFORMATION

Max woke up, the morning sunlight forcing through the inadequate curtains, disturbing his sleep. He had had a wonderful dream about being with the Famous Five on a huge spaceship, flying around the rings of Saturn. Disoriented, he rubbed his eyes and tried to focus. He looked for Brackie, who had completely disappeared. Where could he be? Max checked under the pillows, but he wasn't there, he lifted up the duvet and only saw Matthew, who was stationary at the foot of the bed, he must be tired from playing the night before, Max thought. He got out of bed, and promptly bumped his head on the ceiling with a resounding thud. Dazed and seeing stars, he floundered and winced in pain as his bare foot trampled down on his cherished plastic model Diplodocus. There was an ominous crunching sound, and Max's pain was soon forgotten when he saw with horror that the sauropod's head and neck had broken off.

"Aaah, poor Diplodocus", said Max, cradling the decapitated body. "Never mind, you can easily grow a new head." Max, stooped, padded to the wardrobe and lifted down from on top of it a brand new, boxed Diplodocus, fully intact.

Max was the luckiest boy in the world, an inexhaustible supply of new dinosaurs!

Max felt the urge to pee and crept through to the bathroom, as quietly as a nine foot tall human being can. Despite the thud of head on ceiling and yelp of pain from his dinosaur-imprinted foot, Daddy and Julie were still asleep; he could hear a faint snore as he passed their bedroom. Max stood over the toilet bowl and bent his knees to minimise the aiming distance; this mundane bodily act had become a considerable feat of contortion, but splashes were still routine and a source of angst in the Anderson household.

Afterwards, he washed his hands like a good boy, just like he had been told by Julie (Daddy didn't seem to bother). After a painting session, he had given his hands a cursory rinse and made Julie angry by blackening a hand towel. She had given him a bad tempered hand-washing lesson, and he was now careful to get all the nooks and crannies. On returning to the bedroom Max could see that Matthew was still under the duvet, golly he must be tired! He busied himself setting up another mass battle between the dinosaur meat-eaters and plant-eaters. The veggies would win, as usual, Brackie would deliver the killer blow. Allosaurus, the black and yellow stripy carnivore, would die, again. Max didn't like Allosaurus very much.

After losing himself in the battle for a little while, possibly twenty minutes or so, Max suddenly became puzzled, and looked curiously over at the bed. Something was wrong, and it took Max a few moments to decide what it was. Soon, the penny dropped – Matthew would normally have gone out into the garden by now to do his business. Often he would wake Max up, whining and scratching at the door. Max suddenly panicked – had Matthew made a mess in the bed? Max didn't want to get told off, it wasn't his fault!

He flung off the duvet and looked at Matthew's inert form. "Come on, doggy. Come on, boy". He poked the Dalmatian in the tummy, gently at first, then more firmly. There was no response. Puzzlement was slowly replaced by horror, a gut-wrenching realisation hitting Max in the pit of his stomach like a frozen dagger.

Mark and Julie, spooning, half asleep and happy in a warm, cosy cocoon under the bedclothes, were abruptly jarred out of bed by Max's blood-curdling screams.

46

TIME CHANGER

They rushed Matthew to the veterinary hospital, approximately ten miles away. Mark knew it was futile, but realised that Max had to be satisfied that all possible steps had to be taken to save his beloved companion.

They drove in their "Maxmobile", a specially converted Range Rover with a lowered, reclined seat and extended footwell. This effectively took out the entire front passenger section, and half of the rear passenger seating area. This had been donated by Range Rover themselves, who in turn were responsible for some of the cheesiest Max-related puns in their advertisements. Julie occupied the sole back seat, cradling Matthew's still form.

On arrival at the hospital, the reception staff gave a look of bewildered surprise as Max squeezed himself through the entrance, and shuffled towards the desk in his now characteristic hunched walk. His face was red raw from crying. The staff recognised Max from the television of course, but seeing a nine-foot tall person on a screen and meeting them in the flesh were entirely different experiences.

There was a consultant on emergency duty and she saw

them straight away. A stern-looking woman in her early forties, she sported a white laboratory coat and greying ponytail. She recoiled in surprise at Max, and for a moment, struggled to regain her composure. Her face briefly broke into a polite smile, reverting quickly to her frosty demeanour. "Hello, Mr Anderson," she said, "I'm Brenda Simpson. Please come into the consulting room."

Matthew's death was confirmed within a few minutes of him being examined. Max wailed in despair and disbelief – he'd never known a life without his devoted companion. Nor had he suffered any bereavement. This was a raw, devastating experience for him. Julie led him away to be consoled by a cuddle and whatever he wanted from the vending machine.

Brenda explained, "There would have to be an autopsy to make certain, but my initial assessment is that poor Matthew died of crushing injuries and asphyxia."

"Crushing and asphyxia? What do you mean? How can you tell?"

"At least three broken ribs, burst blood vessels in the eye, blood in the mouth, and, I suspect, internal bleeding, too."

"Oh my God," exclaimed Mark, "that would mean it was Max's fault. He must have rolled over in bed, squashed him or something. That poor dog."

"It's a great tragedy, Mr Anderson, but it was both foreseeable and preventable. Your son – forgive me for speaking up like this, but avoidable animal deaths do rather anger me." The vet took a deep breath and adopted a steely glare, suddenly abandoning her compassionate manner. "Your son should never have been allowed to sleep in the same bed as the dog. It was an accident waiting to happen. You're lucky that Matthew lasted as long as he did, quite frankly."

"But....but they've been inseparable since he was a baby. He must – he must have been unusually tired last night, he must have slept deeply. A dead weight." Mark recalled Max's latest weigh-in and winced – his son now weighed in excess of thirty-two stones. Two hundred kilos!

"If Max is told it was his fault, I'm not sure he'd ever get over it."

Brenda said, angrily, "Mr Anderson, have you seen the size and bulk of your son?" Mark nodded and furrowed his brow, irritated and confused by such an obviously rhetorical question. She went on, "He is the most massive human being that's ever lived. He's a danger to himself and everyone around him. He probably has no idea of his own bulk or strength. That poor dog, as you put it, never stood a chance."

"Now, Brenda, hang on a minute..."

"If you ask me, it will be good for Max to learn a lesson at this young age. He needs to accept that he is an unusual human being. The normal rules simply don't apply – he's got to learn, and learn urgently, that he's got to be ultra-careful at all times. And, I'm afraid one of the consequences of his – condition, is that he must be supervised when he is around animals, not to mention people, and absolutely not, under any circumstances, be allowed to sleep in the same bed as another living creature."

"I was thinking that we would get another dog, Max needs a companion, and they're bound to want to sleep together."

"It's simply out of the question. Now, would you like an autopsy to be performed?"

Mark pondered this for a moment. "No, thank you. I think it's best we have a cremation and try and move forward as quickly as possible. I don't agree that Max needs to learn a hard lesson. He has a life ahead of him that you and I can't really begin to comprehend. The longer I can keep him innocent and happy the better. The dog was getting on for twelve years old – a good average for a Dalmatian – as far as Max will ever know, Matthew died of old age, peacefully in his sleep."

"But that's a lie. The boy has got to learn before something else gets killed, or someone."

"It's a white lie, Dr Simpson." Mark dropped the informality. "You stick to the animals, leave the parenting to me. Now, how do I go about organising a cremation?"

47

WEAR THE CHAINS

Johnny Bird woke up, a gnawing pain from his back thanks to a broken mattress spring. He was cold, uncomfortable and hungry. A dank smell of damp, sweat and disinfectant pervaded his nostrils. Beneath him, a gentle but rasping snore radiated, filling the room. Shit, thought Johnny, never get back to sleep now.

Today was the third anniversary of his incarceration in Leicester prison. He was serving a ten year stretch for possession with intent to supply. A total fit up; yes he had been using, and yes he had shared some of his stash with his girlfriends, but he was no drug dealer! That was obvious, surely – had he really been dealing he would have been maimed or murdered by a rival seller. No, he was just having fun.

Unfortunately, the fuckwitted cops and the clueless twats on the jury hadn't seen it that way. The quantities of E and blow found in his flat were too large for personal recreational use, they said. He must have been dealing.

Johnny had made a fortune out of Bob, Bell and the freak Anderson boy. Awash with unprecedented amounts of cash, he had decided he was going to enjoy himself. Girls, booze, drugs, nothing was beyond his reach. He wasn't hurting anyone, so why did the pigs target his flat for a raid? That was something he would get to the bottom of, when he was out. And while he was at it, he'd expose the police for what they are – a corrupt clique doing favours for their mates and fuck everyone else. They were all freemasons, Johnny supposed. He'll show them – a proper investigative journalism piece, prize-winning stuff. He'd start with that bastard who arrested him, Detective Inspector Perkins. What kind of name was that, anyway? Was anyone really called 'Perkins' these days?

His time in the slammer had not been easy – there was a code of honour amongst the inmate population, and drug-dealing tabloid hacks would never win any popularity contests. He had meals stolen, had his beatings. Johnny had suffered indignities at the hands of the bull queens.

And two weeks ago, his new cell mate had moved in – a tedious former accountant, in for a fraud conviction, and conspiracy to pervert the course of justice. He was as much fun as a wet weekend in Wigan.

So, three years in, two to go, assuming he kept his nose clean and was released on licence halfway through his sentence. In addition to getting his revenge on the cops, there was one thing in particular he would need to focus on to get himself through the time. One big story, one more shattering revelation, one unfinished story he had to complete.

In two years, the world would know all about Maxwell Anderson's twin brother.

48

SON OF MINE

The fact of Matthew's tragic death was matched in its awfulness only by the manner in which it had been caused and the appalling, wretched emotion shown by Max at the short but dignified ceremony at the pet crematorium. They were all affected: Julie, Mark, Shirley and even the normally stoical Roger were deeply moved by the loss of a valued family member and the plight this was causing their beloved Max.

Approaching his eighth birthday, Max's emotional intelligence was underdeveloped, hampered by his relative isolation from human contact. A nine-foot tall youngster, out of school; he had no friends of his own age. Max had not encountered death in any direct or tangible form; he was unable to rationalise the accident or accept that Matthew would never be cuddling up to him in bed ever again. His distress at the cremation pervaded the thoughts of the whole family. Mark, trying to be strong for his son, suppressed his sobs, but his face was a mask of despair.

Sensing the moment, it was clear to Roger that on a raw, human level, his son needed his father now more than ever before. An unfamiliar feeling of parental devotion crawled across his body like poison ivy. Mark needed a break from the tsunami of post-cremation distress that was engulfing his family.

On arrival at the family home, Roger placed a firm hand on Mark's shoulder, allowing Shirley and Julie to lead Max into the house. Max, usually stooped in self-consciousness about his height, was almost doubled over in disconsolate distress.

"Son, you're coming with me," said Roger, in a firm, warm tone which made clear that he simply would not take "no" for an answer. "Come and have a pint with your poor old Dad."

"A pint? What do you mean a pint? We never have 'a pint'. I need to get inside, I've got to help Max..."

"He's in good hands – the women-folk are all over him like a rash. Best thing you can do is put yourself first for a couple of hours. Let someone look after you for a change."

Mark, with trembling lip, wrestled with his conscience; or at least, tried to give the impression of being torn. In fact, although acutely conscious of the need to be seen to be supporting his son, the opportunity to escape from the oppressiveness washed over him like an autumnal sunrise melting away the frost.

At the pub, Roger strode forward to buy the beers. Their footsteps echoed from the bare wooden floorboards and sparse décor. It was the kind of pub where the initial enthusiasm of the incoming proprietors had, a couple of years later, waned; a couple of stubborn regulars chatted to a disinterested forty-something barmaid; she looked older. The Eagles' Greatest Hits were playing on the underpowered speakers of a portable CD player, on a shelf behind the bar.

"One of These Nights" gave way to "Hotel California" as Roger collected their two pints of locally-brewed bitter and they took a table as far away from the other punters as they could find. Mark frowned as the table wobbled annoyingly as Roger placed the beers on its unwiped, beermat-free wooden surface. His frown was soon dispelled; after gulping a few mouthfuls of bitter he allowed himself a slight smile and audible sigh of pleasure.

A few moments of serenity passed between the two men. Remembering why they were there, Roger looked across at his son, an unforced expression of sympathy melted across his face.

"Do you remember the last time we shared a pint, son?"

Mark struggled, momentarily stumped. A flicker of recognition sparked into his eyes. "Twenty-three years ago. My eighteenth birthday. You had this romantic fantasy about bonding over a beer, once I was old enough. You'd done the same with Granddad."

"Well, you know, it's the thing that fathers do with their sons. You'll do the same with Max, when the time comes." Roger averted his gaze from Mark's; both men harboured private doubts that such an event was very unlikely.

They finished their beers in gradual, uncomfortable silence, awkwardly sipping the beers, attempting but not quite succeeding to hasten the process without causing offence by giving the impression of doing so. Neither men could find the words to establish an emotional connection with the other.

Mark certainly appreciated the gesture that Roger was trying to make, but he simply did not have that kind of relationship with his father, and felt that he never would.

He resolved to ensure that he avoided the mistakes of his own father: his own upbringing characterised by Roger's intellectual point-scoring, resentfulness of the financial cost of rearing children; the foisting of his own beliefs on a confused child; the disappointment at Mark's failure to develop the same passions and interests.

Mark vowed to ensure that the bond between him and Max would be unbreakable. Nothing was more important. There are moments in life when a son needs his father. Mark would be there for Max when he needed him most.

49

WE WILL BETTER THE WORLD

Richard Crowe looked up from his binocular microscope and frowned. Now in his early-forties, he had persisted with keeping his hair long, although a receding fringe and greyish tinge gave him the look of a sad aged rock star rather than the brilliant surgeon and scientist he considered himself to be.

He was perched on a bar stool, crouching over a high-set desk in the study-cum-laboratory he had converted for himself in the middle bedroom of his detached bungalow in a small Leicestershire village. On the desk, which spanned the length of one side of the room, were boxes containing microscope slides, petri dishes, the microscope itself, and mounted at one end, a large cuboid piece of machinery with a plethora of control buttons and an LCD display. Each mounted in a silver frame were A4-sized pictures of Robert Wadlow, now the world's second tallest human being, Daniel Lambert, Leicestershire's own giant, and Maxwell Anderson towering over his father.

The walls of the room were lined with bookshelves, medical textbooks and journals in abundance. They were sorted alphabetically by author's surname, and chronologically within each author's grouping. There were two volumes with his own name emblazoned on their spines, both with absurdly lengthy titles typical of the medical reference genre: "Studies into the Proportionality of Organ Development in Cases of Dwarfism and Gigantism" and "The Practicalities and Ethics of Genetic Intervention when Abnormalities are Discovered in the Foetus".

For him, the publication was incidental to the thrill and intrigue of the science. He was driven by the prospect of making a fantastic new discovery, a revolutionary technique that would change the world, secure his name in the annals of history. It was pursuit of the goal that had led him to eschew social and romantic relationships, his single-minded determination filling his spare time with experiments, technical reading and writing. He allowed himself sufficient time to eat, and the occasional wash.

In the gaps between shelves a few posters were displayed, cutaway diagrams each showing a different aspect of the workings of the human body; circulatory, respiratory, brain and nervous system, muscular, digestive, reproductive and skeletal. A small tiny radio was playing his favourite classical music station. A Beethoven piano sonata was currently playing.

In the corner of the room was a human corpse, perfectly embalmed and preserved, the handiwork of an unorthodox and unethical mortician. The corpse was of an adult male midget, who had donated his body to medical science, without realising that his destiny was to be stuffed and mounted rather than dissected and analysed.

In the earlier part of his research career, he had struggled to obtain funding for his work from any legitimate source. He had been forced to use illicit channels to obtain tissue samples for experimentation. Such work would rarely yield useful results, and he would always crave the opportunity to test his theories on a live subject.

And then from out of nowhere, about ten years previously, the planners of Project Scorpio had approached him. Intrigued by his earlier published works, he apparently had exactly the right expertise they were looking for. He was the one man who could translate the theoretical concepts into practical reality. He would be forever remembered as one of the true pioneers of human genetic engineering. And he would be guaranteed access to whatever physical and financial resources were necessary to deliver the Project's objectives. Failures would be tolerated provided that demonstrable progress was made. Agreeing to participate was a straightforward decision. He had been obliged to formally acknowledge that absolute discretion was required, and there would be consequences if this was not observed.

Crowe consulted his notebook, and inscribed a few more scribbled notes. He substituted the slide he had been scrutinising for another from his box, and peered back into the eyepieces. Maybe, he thought, today he will discover how to reliably replicate the Maxwell Anderson phenomenon. Just because there had been many grotesque failures since, it did not mean that his success with Maxwell was a fluke.

50

THE OUTSIDER

Shortly after moving in to their new custom built facility, Mark decided to throw a house-warming party. Roger and Shirley were there of course, refreshed and in good humour having just returned from a Mediterranean cruise to celebrate his sixty-fifth birthday and retirement.

Mark's sister Marie also attended, accompanied by her civil partner, Claire. There was still a frisson of awkwardness around Claire; Shirley in particular apparently struggling to come to terms with "how things had turned out". Claire was a highly paid project manager, working in the construction industry, and was accustomed to overcoming scepticism and prejudice through her brisk, direct and efficient manner. Today she was wearing a tartan-patterned shirt, tight jeans and new Reebok trainers; her hair dyed black with purple highlights above a pale complexion and bright blue eyes. Mark fancied her, actually, but would not admit as much to Julie, who had bonded well with Claire, and looked forward to their occasional visits. It was clear to everyone that Marie was happy, which was the most important thing, after all.

Freddie Abbott arrived, characteristically late, but at least he turned up, Mark thought. Flashy as ever, he had driven up in a Morgan classic sports car, with his latest young dolly bird girlfriend, Sasha. His dealership had continued to prosper despite the economic turbulence of the past few years. Rich people stay rich even in a crisis, and could still afford luxurious extravagances. These people were his customer base, not the squeezed middle or the impoverished. Mark and Freddie saw each other increasingly infrequently as time wore on, perhaps once a year or every eighteen months or so. But this meant that there was always plenty to catch up on, and Freddie was always startled to see the change in Max after such a length of time. The hairs had stood up on the back of his neck when he saw that Max was now a little over nine feet tall. Sasha, spooked and obviously unprepared, rather tactlessly ran back outside, and lit a cigarette. Fortunately, Max had become accustomed to this kind of reaction.

When Max was safely out of earshot, Freddie said, "Good grief, Marky, what the bloody hell are you going to do if this doesn't stop?"

"Mate, I've absolutely no idea whatsoever. Not the slightest clue. I'm scared shitless, to be honest."

Also at the party were Ralph, Christine, and a few of Julie's colleagues, most of them former workmates of Mark's. It was good to see them again.

Bob and Bell were not invited.

The new house was actually a bungalow. Each doorway was ten feet high and five feet wide, power assisted doors opening and closing automatically, albeit irritatingly slowly, by means of a keypad or detection of a proximity card worn about the person. Each door had its own customised programming; there were times when Mark and Julie needed privacy without their bedroom door suddenly opening.

The ceilings in each room had a twelve feet clearance. A single corridor ran through the house, from which each room was accessed. From the front entrance, the first room on the left was Max's bathroom, equipped with custom built outsized lavatory, bath, shower cubicle, washbasin and mirror. Max's bedroom was next. His bed was twelve feet by six. One wall was taken up by a clothes rail, the latest creations by Four X Fashions all on display. A fifty-inch plasma television was mounted on another wall, connected to a switchbox that easily enabled an eight-year old's mind to select between TV, DVD, Internet and games console. On the third wall was a massive, specially constructed cabinet that was home to Max's beloved collection of dinosaur figurines, Brackie in pride of place front and centre. Books and DVDs occupied the remaining wall on shelves above a writing desk on which sat a computer and monitor. The room was completed by a painter's easel, although Max had shown little interest in art since Matthew died.

Mark's bedroom was next, still with enormous doorway and high ceiling, but with conventional furniture. Julie had her own wardrobe and cabinet, but had still not moved in permanently. Mark thought that he may have to up the ante on that soon.

The kitchen diner had worktops and cupboards at a height accessible for Max, which meant that Mark and Julie needed to make use of an elephant's foot to reach what they need. The table was also built so that Max could sit comfortably on his oversized chair; the other chairs ingeniously incorporated little steps so that people of regular height could join Max on his own level. The experience was a little like climbing up into a lorry driver's cab, Mark thought. On the table were drinks, glasses and nibbles for the party.

Off the kitchen was the utility room, dominated by three industrial washing machines and three dryers. At least one of each was permanently in action to cope with demands that Max, with all the dirty habits of any young boy, would generate. Finally, the living room, with Max-sized sofa and armchairs, enabled a cosy family gathering of an evening. French doors opened out to a newly landscaped garden, freshly turfed and surrounded by a twelve foot fence to give Max some semblance of privacy from inquisitive neighbours and press photographers.

"Do you think you can be happy here, Mark?" asked Ralph, sidling up with a glass of sparkling wine.

"It's wonderful, thank you Ralph. We weren't coping in my old house. And you made it possible, of course. And Max loves it. No more crash helmet!"

"He's turning into a fine young man, your son. Anyway, I've got something to talk with you about - an "at home" photo spread for either Hello or OK magazines - waiting to see who will bid the most. Could be enough to build you a home cinema, or snooker room."

"No, a hot tub is first on the list. Sounds good - we'll chat later, when people have gone."

Mark thought to himself, yes, we can be happy here. If Max stops growing.

But what if he doesn't? What the Hell am I going to do?

Shuddering, Mark returned to the party. Despite having his friends and family around him, and the woman he loved, Mark suddenly felt like the loneliest person on Earth.

51

IT'S NOT TOO LATE

A few days after the housewarming, Mark was at home, idly flicking through the channels. Julie was at work. God, daytime TV is shite, he thought, as he weighed up the respective merits of an antiques show, a cookery programme, a chat show which seemed to have been designed exclusively for the enjoyment of screaming morons, horse racing or an Australian soap.

Mark increasingly found himself at a loose end these days – there had been a persistent flurry of activity for the past few years, working with Ralph to secure appropriately sensitive and lucrative media coverage, and subsequently, commercial sponsorship and endorsement contracts. Coping with Max was now much more manageable as a result, and Mark was grateful. However, with media interest waning, and having given up on his career, Mark was bored.

Max was in his bedroom, with Christine. What a rock she had become; she was now firmly part of the family, as far as Mark was concerned. Max adored her, and responded well to her tutelage. He had acquired a keen interest in history and science, and developed an aptitude for English and maths, although the latter was not his strength and did not come naturally. The only blip in the home schooling was the absence of socialisation opportunities, which Mark was worried could cause Max problems in later life, when his interactions with other people would never be straightforward. Physical Education was also lacking, and Max had lost interest in his art. He would speak with Christine about other non-academic activity, so that Max could have a break from poring over workbooks. Maybe music?

As the horse racing gave way to Countdown, something which Mark could at least derive some intellectual stimulation from, Christine came into the living room. She had recently switched from wearing thick glasses to contact lenses, and was dressing more smartly then she used to. She looked several years younger than her fifty-three years, and if she would only do something with her short, curly hair, would actually be quite attractive.

"Well, that's it for another day!" she said, cheerily.

"Excellent thank you. Before you go, Chris, there's something I wanted to pick your brains about."

"Actually, Mark, there's something I wanted to discuss with you."

"Oh, really?" He affected a casual air, suddenly dreading what Christine was about to say. She's not resigning, surely? We don't want yet another upheaval, not now!

"Yes, it's about Max. He's not been himself since he lost Matthew. The best way I can describe it is – the spark has gone. He's not engaging with lessons with his usual enthusiasm, and he's hardly doing any homework at the moment."

"Have you asked him what the matter is?"

"Yes, of course, but he just says 'nothing', or that he misses Matthew. Mark, I think there's something troubling him. He's almost nine years old, and he's increasingly aware of his emotions, feelings, and the fact he is different from everyone else."

"I see. What do you suggest?"

"I think he needs a good old heart to heart with his Dad. Get to the bottom of what's eating away at him."

"OK, I will. Thanks, Christine. You do know he's very fond of you, don't you? As am I."

"Yes, I think so. I don't think any of this is personal towards me. Have a talk with your son. Anyway, goodnight – I'll see myself out. Oh, and Mark?"

"Yes?"

"The feeling's mutual by the way."

52

I AM YOUR FATHER

Mark decided to leave Max a little space, and continued watching Countdown. Rick Wakeman was in Dictionary Corner. Mark had long been a fan, not just of his music, but also his curmudgeonly wit and cutting sense of humour. He was in fine form on today's show. As usual, Mark failed to compete effectively with the contestants, especially on the numbers rounds.

He walked along the corridor and stood in Max's bedroom doorway, taking a moment to regard his son. He was playing a video game, some sort of futuristic racer, but not doing very well. He was struggling to manipulate the console's control pad effectively, the buttons not designed for supersized fingers. Max was getting frustrated and upset. After one more crash, Max threw the control pad down in disgust.

"Hello, son. How are you getting on?"

"Rubbish. Can't steer prop'ly. Can't press the buttons."

"Oh, dear. We'll see if we can get bigger buttons. Meanwhile, keep trying, you'll get the hang of it."

"Don't want to."

"How was your day, son? What did you learn today?"

"Not much. Today was boring. Christine was boring."

Mark took a deep breath. Christine was right – this was not like Max. Something was clearly bothering him.

"Max, you do know that Daddy loves you very much, yes?" Max grunted an acknowledgement, and picked up a couple of dinosaur toys. Dimetrodon and Protoceratops, Mark thought, uncertainly. They looked small in Max's immense palms. He continued, "and Julie, too? And Grandad and Grandma? We all love you. And we'll always be here for you, whenever you have a problem, we're all here to help."

Max continued playing, ignoring Mark.

"Max, look at me," he said, firmly. His son looked up. Tears were forming in his eyes. "Max, what's wrong. Please tell me. Daddy will do his very best to help. I promise."

"Why me?"

Mark recoiled, unsure what to make of the question. "Why you? Sorry, Max, I don't know what you mean?" Although, of course, he did really.

"Why am I different, Daddy?"

"Well, Max, everybody is different. Everyone has something about them that makes them special. You're special, too."

"But why am I so big? Why can't I be normal?"

"Honestly Max, I don't know. Obviously God decided that there needed to be a big person, and that you should be the one."

"But it's just not FAIR. I can't go to school. I can't have friends. I can't play video games prop'ly. I can't have any more doggies."

"I know it feels tough now, son, but it just means that you were meant to do special things. You will feel better about this when you're older." As he was speaking, Mark realised he was failing to provide the inspirational reassurance that Max was looking for. He cursed himself, this was a conversation he should have anticipated, and prepared for.

"Will I have a Mummy when I'm older, Daddy? Other children have Mummies. Why haven't I got one?"

"Well, Max, you know the answer to this one. Mummy is in Heaven. We've talked about this. Mummy can't be with you. Instead, you have me....and Julie. You like Julie, don't you?"

"Julie's nice. But she's not my Mummy. Why did Mummy go to Heaven? Was it my fault, just like it was my fault that Matthew went to Heaven?"

"No, of course not." Shit, thought Mark, who had Max been talking to? He had never blamed his son for Matthew's death. Unless he had worked it out for himself, he was a bright boy. My God, what a guilt trip that poor boy must be going through. And where has all this stuff about Melanie come from? Was this Christine's doing?

"Well, it's just NOT FAIR," repeated Max. I want to be a normal boy with normal friends, and a normal house, and a normal Mummy." He was crying now. "I hate God. God is nasty. It's NOT FAIR!"

The more this goes on, thought Mark, grimly, the more I'm convinced that God has got absolutely nothing to do with it.

53

THE CONCLUSION

Caroline Harris strode hurriedly along Whitehall, anxious for her appearance not to be too messed up by the shower which had inconveniently decided to fall at this precise moment. She had stupidly left her brolly at her desk in the Home Office. She was keen to impress at her first ever meeting with the Prime Minister, and being self-conscious about her dishevelled, damp hair and sodden outfit were things she could not afford to worry about. This was her chance to catapult herself into 'high-flyer' status; to make her mark.

These days, there were targets and quotas for women in each grade of the Civil Service, but these were rarely met and in practice a cliquey closed shop operated in many Government departments. Caroline often thought of the classic TV moment in which the Minister, Jim Hacker MP, instructed that 'something MUST be done about the number of women in the Civil Service!' only for the dapper Permanent Secretary Sir Humphrey Appleby to answer 'oh, surely there can't be all that many?' More than thirty years later, misogynists still ruled.

Caroline had been rather lucky, though, to serve in a

department run by a female Permanent Secretary, and for the past two years, a female Home Secretary as well. Now thirty-three, she had been working in the Home Office since graduating with honours in Sociology eleven years previously. Hard working, serious and effective, she was still single despite having a slim figure and attractive, gazelle-like appearance, dominated by long, fulsome auburn hair. She had earned regular promotions, helped by the PermSec's strong personal interest in her career. Or possibly, an interest in her personally, she sometimes mused.

For the past three years she had been running the Media Monitoring Division, which existed to identify items of unusual public interest, to analyse their implications for Home Office policy and national security, and to make recommendations to Ministers. She had been tracking the Maxwell Anderson phenomenon, and had written several briefing papers on the cultural, social and political implications. At last, the Personal Private Secretary to whom she directly reported had supported her in attracting the attention of the Junior Minister. In quick succession, the Secretary of State and now the Prime Minister himself were suddenly interested. A conference had been called for this afternoon, at which Caroline was due to play a starring role.

Bustling past a group of Japanese tourists, she approached the black metal gates at the entrance to Downing Street. She presented her official Home Office identification and appointment confirmation letter to the police sentry, slightly unnerved to see that his colleagues were in body armour and carrying what appeared to be light sub-machine guns.

After passing through the metal detector she was

cheerily waved through onto the Street. It was apparently deserted; no phalanx of photographers, no BBC political reporters and apparently no more police beyond the security cordon. She had little doubt, though, that if an incident was to occur, the place would be swarming with officers in an instant.

She walked past the row of ordinary terraced houses which the exterior of Downing Street still resembled. She was aware that, in fact, Number Ten itself was several buildings knocked through into one complex. Approaching the iconic entrance, she was surprised to see that not only was the famous front door open, there was no external police presence. She walked into the building unimpeded. A quick look left and right confirmed that a corridor existed linking the adjoining houses to Number Ten itself. A cadaverous man of about sixty intercepted her, courteously asked her to surrender her smartphone, and briskly escorted her to a small wood-panelled meeting room at the rear of the house. She was disappointed not to be meeting in the Cabinet Room itself, or to have a chance to climb the familiar central staircase, lined with portraits of past-Prime Ministers.

Already in the room were the Home Secretary herself, fresh from the preceding Cabinet Sub-Committee; the Cabinet Secretary, every inch the archetypal mandarin, grey-haired, late fifties, dark suited with waistcoat; and the Prime Minister's Personal Private Secretary, a younger man tapping away busily at a laptop.

"Ah, Ms Harris, welcome," oozed the Permanent Secretary, charming, emollient and unctuous. "Please help yourself to a hot drink. The PM will be here momentarily."

"Hello, Caroline, thanks for coming," said the Home

Secretary. She sidled up to Caroline and whispered, conspiratorially, "Don't worry, he's in a good mood today. Be yourself, you'll storm it!"

They sat down at the oblong meeting table. Caroline officiously studied the briefing note that had been circulated, although she could probably recite it verbatim; she had written it, after all. She decided against initiating small talk with the others, wisely concentrating on the key messages and suggestions she wanted to get across.

Abruptly, the Prime Minister swept into the room. He was tall, wearing John Lennon glasses and almost completely bald, in the way that made it hard to gauge his age, although Caroline was aware he was fifty-one. She felt a slight quiver of excitement, there was an undeniable aura when someone of such importance was in such close proximity. She felt herself reddening.

There was no pre-amble, no attempt to break the ice. "People," said the Prime Minister in his familiar deep Lancastrian tone, "Maxwell Anderson has to be brought in. He has to be studied."

54

CUTTHROAT ISLAND

All prisons have rules which must be obeyed, or there will be consequences. Obviously, to be incarcerated in the first place, society's rules will have been broken, assuming there has been no miscarriage of justice. Once inside, there is an official regime of prison discipline. The Governor, using national guidelines as a framework, will prescribe a routine that permeates all day to day aspects of the inmates' lives. When to get up, when to sleep. When to wash and shave. When to eat, when to exercise. Visiting rights. What TV channels to watch, what books and magazines to read, what websites to look at. Standards of behaviour towards fellow inmates, and in particular, warders and prison staff. Transgressing any of these rules results in punishment; revocation of privileges, solitary confinement. The threat of an unofficial and highly illegal beating by the warders was usually enough to keep people in line.

But the rules that matter most in prison, the ones that could literally determine if someone lives or dies, are the unwritten ones. Honour amongst thieves; there is a code of ethics that even the most hardened criminals abide by, if they want to live. It is this code that forces paedophiles to be segregated for their own safety. More commonly, the code dictates the hierarchy of power among the inmate community; the Made Men, the people who do their bidding, the downtrodden minority. And the code says that you must not, under any circumstances whatsoever, steal from a fellow prisoner. Theft of the items most needed for sanity behind prison walls – food, booze, cigarettes, drugs, porn, cell phones – is regarded as unforgiveable. And there will be consequences if you disobey.

Johnny's fraudster cellmate, Antony, although somewhat dull, was a devious son of a bitch. He had worked out who to befriend, which inmates could be influenced, which guys had access to incoming materials, legitimate or contraband. He had provided a few sexual favours. All of this enabled Antony to enjoy more than his fair share of prison life's small pleasures. And, to make the twenty hours a day spent cooped up with his cellmate more bearable, Antony had offered to share some of his illicitly obtained booty with Johnny.

After more than two years of enforced abstinence and celibacy, Johnny had begun to crave new ways to make the time stretching ahead of him more bearable. He did not enjoy Antony's company. So the offer of a stash of pot, Glenfiddich and an unused Penthouse magazine magazine came as an unexpected but most welcome surprise, which Johnny gratefully received.

After a couple of months of Johnny accepting regular gifts from his new best friend, and some enjoyable spliff-fuelled conversations, the supplies abruptly stopped. One of the prison bosses, nobody official of course, this boss was a Made Man with a brigade of loyal henchmen, had discovered why he hadn't received his monthly bottle of single malt. Antony's main source of goods, Patrick, a younger prisoner with cleaning duties which included the mailroom, was found badly beaten and dead in a communal shower. He had been suffocated; there was a bar of soap jammed into his windpipe.

Word travels fast in prison. And the word was that Patrick had squealed before he was killed. He had named the people who had bribed and coerced him into intercepting the incoming smuggled goods. It would only be a short time before the Made Men decided the fate of Patrick's trading partners, and gave the inevitable instructions to their lieutenants.

Antony's days were numbered. And that meant that Johnny was now on borrowed time, too. For the first time since a young boy, sent to bed early for truanting from school, Johnny cried himself to sleep.

55

LIFELINE

Caroline Harris was under pressure. The Home Secretary was demanding to know why the research facility was not yet operational, and was not yet occupied by the person it was designed for. Number Ten was impatient. It was now more than six months since the Prime Minister had issued instructions that Maxwell Anderson must be studied.

Caroline, Home Office high flier and personal favourite of the Permanent Secretary, had been assigned to manage this project. She had to find a suitable building that could be adapted into a suitable scientific research facility, and she needed the personnel with the knowledge and expertise to design the laboratory and operate it to produce meaningful insights into the phenomenon. All in the strictest secrecy, of course.

At no stage did the project – codename Operation Scorpio – progress straightforwardly. It had taken as long as seven weeks to find the suitable site, a disused military aircraft hangar on a former RAF airfield. The site was still owned by the Ministry of Defence, but Government departments rarely co-operated quickly with one another. It had taken Prime Ministerial intervention to get the MoD wheels turning. Sourcing an architect capable of designing a layout for the hangar building that included living quarters for a nine feet tall human being was especially problematic. Then the adaptation works themselves had to be commissioned, and this was all before the scientific side of the project could be initiated.

Fortunately, one step in the process did go remarkably smoothly. Caroline, acting under full Ministerial authority, obtained the career history and medical credentials of all practising private and NHS doctors in the country. In electronic form, it had not been particularly time consuming to filter out a shortlist of appropriately qualified experts.

At the interviews, Caroline did not reveal the nature of the assignment, but did inform the candidates that they were being considered for a very special position as a Government scientific adviser, and it was potentially a career-defining role. When she told people that the assignment entailed absolute confidentiality, with the appointee being bound by the Official Secrets Act with serious consequences of breaching that trust, a few candidates withdrew from the recruitment process.

Fortunately, this did not matter. Caroline was immediately impressed by one candidate in particular. Someone with exactly the qualifications and experience they were looking for. Someone with a proven track record of delivering tangible scientific results within the relevant field. Someone with unfulfilled ambitions to make an even greater contribution. A person whom Caroline felt would be a natural leader of the science team. A candidate who was head and shoulders above the other people under consideration. Such was the passion and conviction in which

Caroline expressed these views, the other members of the panel put aside their own concerns about the candidate's suitability, especially his lack of personal charm, and they deferred to her view.

Yes, the panel were pleased to offer the assignment to their ideal candidate. They were not nearly so delighted, however, as Doctor Richard Crowe. He accepted the appointment without hesitation.

56

BROKEN HOMES

Mark did not feel like organising any celebrations for Max's tenth birthday, but Julie persuaded him that an occasion needed to be made of it. Now six inches beyond the Wadlow limit, at nine feet five inches tall, no-one could be sure how many birthdays Max had left. Mark realised it was high time he organised a full medical examination for his son, it was no good assuming that Max's innards were growing healthily and in proportion to the rest of his body.

And Max needed cheering up – the death of Matthew was continuing to hit him hard, even several months later. He had refused Mark's suggestions of getting a new dog. Max continued to blame himself for the accident, and "Why me?" soul searching was now a regular conversation. The "it's God's will" explanation was no longer giving effective solace, if it ever did.

Max was actually starting to outgrow even the new house and its deliberately outsized dimensions: the doorways at ten feet tall were fast becoming too small. Makeshift but conspicuous "Max –Duck!" notices now hung from each doorframe, a permanent, upsetting reminder to Max that he was abnormal.

The rate of growth was such that clothes and shoes continued to have a short useful life. Four X Fashions were beginning to get awkward about the amount of free supplies they were obliged to supply under the endorsement contract. Ralph was on the case, but it seemed inevitable that Mark would have to submit Max to more publicity in order to ensure their key supplier's continued goodwill. He was not sure that Max was in the right frame of mind to co-operate. Yet another thing to worry about.

Roger, Shirley and Christine had dutifully visited for the birthday 'party', but the mood was sombre and atmosphere tense, like a working lunch of interview candidates going for the same job. Part of the problem was getting presents that Max would enjoy and could practically use. The sponsorship deals meant that he had all the toys he was interested in, and of course he had very little companionship with which he could play games. DVDs and books seemed to be the default solution, but Max hadn't been particularly interested in the selection he had received earlier that day.

They were just attempting to inject some jocularity by beginning a game of charades – this was Shirley's suggestion – when Mark heard a few thuds outside – car doors being shut, he supposed – then there was a crisp knocking at the door. Saved by the bell, Mark thought, the knocking rescuing him from having to act out "The Muppet Christmas Carol".

His proximity card activated the front door and it swung silently inward, maddeningly slowly as usual. Standing outside was a smartly dressed woman in her mid-thirties, Mark assumed, with long flowing brown hair. Accompanying her was a large, muscular man in a too-tight suit. He wore an earpiece connected to some unseen equipment by a translucent curly cable. On the road was a large black van, unmarked and with tinted windows, and a black Jaguar saloon car. For an instant, Mark wondered if he was about to be kidnapped by the American Secret Service.

It was the woman who spoke first, "Mr Anderson, my name is Caroline Harris. It's very good to meet you." She offered her hand to Mark, who declined to shake it. Unperturbed, Caroline continued. "We work for the Home Office."

"Who is it, son?" asked Roger, who had joined Mark in the hallway.

"I'm not sure," said Mark, and turned to the strangers outside. "Home Office? What's this about?"

Caroline said, "We're here to help. The Prime Minister and Home Secretary are very interested in Maxwell. They would like to meet him – in fact, there are many of us who would all like to get to know him better. May we see him?"

"No, you may not. What's going on? Why are you here?"

It was the large man who replied, in a surprisingly light voice for someone with so much brawn. "We're here, Mr Anderson, to invite you and your son to join us at a special facility where Maxwell can receive the care and treatment he needs."

"Max doesn't need any treatment. He's perfectly fine here, thank you very much. Now will you please leave?"

The man continued, "I'm afraid you don't understand. We're here by direct Prime Ministerial authority. The Government intends to study your son. It will be simplest if you co-operate."

"Now, look here! Who do you think you are?" demanded Roger.

Caroline said, "As I said, Mr Anderson," acknowledging Roger, "we're from the Home Office. We're here to collect Maxwell, and take him to our special facility. You're welcome to accompany him, of course. Maxwell will be quite safe, in fact he'll receive everything he needs."

Mark pointed at Caroline's companion. "He said that you intend to study my son. What do you mean? On whose authority?"

"As we tried to explain, we're here on the express instructions of the Prime Minister himself. We quite understand your reluctance. But there really is nothing to worry about." She gave a supportive smile. "Would you like half an hour to collect your things?"

"And if I refuse?"

"I'm afraid that really isn't an option. We'll leave in half an hour."

Mark's head started to swim. He felt his mind wading through sticky, viscous slime, struggling to comprehend the situation, body paralysed. He opened his mouth to protest, but no words could form. A thought flashed into his mind. Here and now was a situation in which his son needed his father's help. And yet, with the pressure on, he turned to jelly.

Suddenly, Caroline's eyes widened, and the agent bristled, steeling himself. "My God," he mumbled.

Max lumbered up the hallway, shuffling hesitantly with a pronounced stoop. He joined his father and grandfather at the front door. "Are you here for my birthday party? We're playing charades. I'm winning."

Caroline swallowed, the colour draining from her face. It was one thing reading about Max and seeing him on a screen. But to meet the gargantuan form of a ten year old boy, towering over everyone, at least half as big again as everyone here – was an awe-inspiring, unsettling experience.

"H-Hello, Maxwell. I'm Caroline. We're going for a ride. You can bring some birthday cake, if you like."

Movement caught Mark's eye and he saw three figures emerge from the black van. There were two burly men, seemingly identical to the one who had joined Caroline at the front door. These people mean business – there's serious muscle power here, and they're probably armed, thought Mark grimly. The third figure to emerge made Mark's blood turn to ice. He was instantly recognisable, though several years had passed. The same annoying ponytail, and that unmistakeable, angular nose. Mark had hoped never again to cast eyes upon Doctor Richard Crowe.

57

MOVING IN MY HEART

Max was feeling car-sick, or to be more accurate, van-sick. There were no windows inside the black van. Max was strapped onto a horizontal shelf that ran the entire length down one side of the rear of the van. Max's feet were towards the back of the van, his head adjacent to the driver's compartment.

He was crying.

As he tilted his head to the right he could see that facing him were four seats, the middle two occupied by his Daddy and the new lady, Caroline. Either side were two of the mean men who had earlier led them from the house and into the van itself.

The van was moving. Max couldn't tell how fast they were going, but he could see Daddy and the other people sometimes lurched forward and sometimes bracing themselves against the inertial forces being exerted. He whimpered as his tummy did somersaults.

There had been time to grab a couple of suitcases full of clothes, and some of his favourite toys. Brackie was somewhere in one of the cases. A box set of Willard Price adventure novels, a birthday present from Grandpa and Grandma had also been gathered up.

"Where are we going Daddy? How much longer? I feel sick." He sobbed.

Mark turned to Caroline and demanded, voice raised to combat the vehicle noise, "How far?"

"Another hour. We're going to an old RAF base in Lincolnshire."

Mark turned to his son. "About an hour, Max, not too long. Don't feel sick now, that's just a new car smell you're feeling. Just concentrate on Daddy and we'll be there before we know it."

Max was confused. "But where are we going? And why aren't we going in the Maxmobile, Daddy?"

"It's okay, son, it's all part of the surprise. Just enjoy the ride, if you can." It's a hell of a surprise for me, too, thought Mark.

Mark had a thousand questions for Caroline and had even more threats to make about their treatment and what he would do to them if they weren't released immediately. This was kidnapping, after all. However, if he began berating her, or gave the impression he was in any way angry or frightened, Max was sure to pick up on it. He didn't want to add to the anxiety that his son must already be feeling.

Although startled by what had happened and inwardly furious about the way his family had been invaded, Mark had been curious for some time that the authorities had shown little interest in Max. His son was the largest human being that had ever existed, and was a national media sensation. It was surely inevitable that at some stage in Max's life, he would attract official scrutiny. In fact, Mark was amazed that their family had been unmolested for as long as they had.

Trying to consider the situation objectively, in some

ways he could understand why the agents had turned up out of the blue and coerced them into the van. Clearly, Max was deemed of national importance, and they couldn't leave things to chance. He liked to think that given advance notice and explanation of what the Government intended, he would have co-operated.

He had also begun to quietly despair about Max's condition. Still growing, at this rate Max would soon be ten feet tall, well on the way to outgrowing their new home, supposedly custom-built and specially adapted. They had all assumed that the growth HAD to stop, especially now the Wadlow limit had been breached. So sure were they, no forward thinking had been done about what to do if Max continued expanding. There was no Plan B. Mark was cursing himself for not proactively seeking support, or at the very least, doing some scenario planning. He regretted not maintaining a good relationship with Geoffrey Kelly.

Or Richard Crowe. That was not a welcome development. In Mark's mind Crowe was the person most directly responsible for the plight he and his son now found themselves in. Clearly, when Max was a precariously tiny new baby, Crowe had recklessly tested a new treatment on him, apparently designed to reverse the dwarfism. Something had clearly gone badly wrong, and Crowe was to blame. Mark was sure of that. And now, nine years later, Crowe was back. Mark could only hope and pray that Crowe was now less reckless, more competent, and perhaps had developed a reliable treatment, a remedy that would stop Max growing. It would not be possible to lose any height, but the least Crowe could do is stop it in its tracks.

Mark looked over at Max, bewildered and fearful, still

sobbing and strapped to the shelf like a piece of cargo. Mark suddenly felt an overwhelming desire to cuddle his son, to tell him everything would be okay, Daddy would look after him. Eyes welling up with tears, Mark told himself that above all, he loved his son deeply.

And he would do anything to keep him safe. Anything at all.

58

ANOTHER WORLD

Eventually, the van began to shake and rattle, its suspension jarring over a badly maintained road. Max's watery eyes widened in puzzlement, his reddened face registering alarm.

"It's okay, Max, we're nearly there, hold on, son," soothed Mark.

Caroline's ear was pressed to her cell phone, she was nodding, apparently taking instructions.

Finally the van eased to a halt. Shortly afterwards, Mark heard another vehicle pull up and stop, the black Jaguar, he supposed. He heard footsteps approach the van. Abruptly, the panel door swished open. The daylight was fading; it was now early evening. Mark enjoyed the blast of fresh air, although there was a slight chill.

The tight-suited agent (Mark still didn't know his name) was standing by the van. "Welcome to our facility, Mr Anderson, and Maxwell of course. Please follow me."

Mark reached across to unfasten Max's restraints. "Are we there yet, Daddy?" his son asked. Mark nodded, and smoothed the hair from across Max's face. It was not a straightforward process for Max, muscles cramped from the journey, to extricate himself from the van. He banged his head and screamed out in pain. Mark held his hand and gently shushed him. "Be brave, son," he said. Roger's conditioning. Mark silently cursed himself. Wasn't he supposed to be avoiding the mistakes his own father had made?

They stepped out onto a poorly maintained tarmacked area. As Caroline had said, this was a disused airfield. It was a barren, featureless site; if Mark had not known better he would have thought he was in a desolate part of Russia. The landscape was flat as far as the eye could see. Huge expanses of concrete were punctuated by untidy clumps of untended grass and weeds. A tall wire fence encircled the site's perimeter. About a hundred yards from the van, ominous and foreboding in the creeping twilight, was what from the outside at least, appeared to be a large hangar, towering above the rest of the site like a haunted gothic cathedral. It was the type of hangar large enough to accommodate multiple airliners, with many functional areas and facilities built into its superstructure. Mark could see a few official-looking vehicles parked outside, and several people buzzing about. A small group was stood watching the new arrivals, eager to see their new assignment up close and personal.

The agent, accompanied by Richard Crowe, Caroline and a couple of uniformed men, strode towards the hangar. A sudden thought struck Mark; why not get back into the van and drive it away? They could get a decent head start before their captors, and that is what Mark had begun to think of them as, could begin their chase. After a few seconds of reasoning Mark accepted the futility of such a gesture. The Government had decided to study Max, and would not give up just because of a token show of resistance. The best way Mark could help his son was to make the process as trouble-free as possible. He continued to hold Max's hand and from a distance, any observer would have thought they resembled any father taking his young son for a walk. Such an observer would be stunned to discover that it was the father who was the significantly smaller figure. Mark was now almost four feet shorter than his ten-year old son.

As they approached the hangar, more people had joined the group waiting, there was now about twenty people gathered. Mark was conscious of an excited murmuring and at least one exclamation, "Oh my God! He's real!"

"Who are all these people?" he asked Caroline.

"They're all Home Office personnel, really good people. All carefully selected and specially trained. They'll be taking care of Max. There'll be time for introductions later."

The group's astonished eyes and open mouths followed Max and Mark as they were led up to the hangar. Once wide open to allow aircraft in and out, the hangar had now been sealed with a featureless metal frontispiece. On the right hand side was a recessed panel, about twelve feet high by six wide. It slowly rolled upwards, like an outsized garage door, to reveal the entrance to the facility. Dazzling white light shone out from within.

As Mark entered, his colossal son at his side, his mind raced to recall what this situation reminded him of. It did not take long for the iconic finale of the alien encounter movie, Close Encounters of the Third Kind, to pop into his head. A man, holding hands with a small alien humanoid, silhouetted against the brilliant light, advancing nervously to be swallowed by the mysterious spacecraft.

"Welcome to Project Scorpio", said Caroline, as the doorway rolled shut behind them.

"Daddy, I want to go home," complained Max.

"So do I, son. So do I."

59

THE ANGELS WILL REMEMBER

SLAIN:
EX-MAIL REPORTER KILLED IN JAIL REVENGE ATTACK
by Mail reporter, Ian Steele

Former Mail reporter Johnny Bird was brutally stabbed to death in Leicester prison last night in what appears to be a cold-blooded act of retaliation. Prison bosses said today that Mr Bird was suspected of involvement in handling property stolen from other inmates.

Bird, 32, was serving a sentence for drug dealing, an offence which cut short a promising journalistic career. He was best known for producing the original Mail exclusives about Maxwell Anderson, the young boy with superhuman growth.

After a spell as lead writer for the Mail's home and garden supplement, Bird collaborated with relatives of Maxwell Anderson to publish a book on the boy giant, an act which tore apart the Anderson family. His fall from grace came shortly afterwards, when police found a large quantity of cocaine and ecstasy in his home.

The case later caused a scandal when the arresting officer, Detective Inspector Nicholas Perkins, was revealed by the Mail to be the brother of the Anderson family's manager and media representative, Ralph Perkins.

Said a prison spokesman, "Johnny Bird was found at 7pm last night with serious knife wounds to the throat. A doctor was called and Mr Bird was tragically pronounced dead at the scene. The police have launched an immediate investigation, and are pursuing a line of enquiry that Mr Bird was murdered because of his alleged participation in the theft of goods from other prisoners. We extend our condolences to Mr Bird's friends and family."

Bird's murder is the seventh in England's jails this year and has fuelled emerging concerns about the escalation of knife crime within the country's prisons. The Home Office said it was unable to comment on specific cases, but was doing all it could to make prisons safer.

60

TIME HAS COME TODAY

The Leader screwed up his eye sockets to grip the eyepieces of the binoculars. This did not improve the view, but somehow he felt that it did. He watched intently as the object of his devotions was swallowed whole by the metal orifice. Anger swelled inside him and he kicked backwards against the people carrier he was leaning against, leaving an untidy dent in the driver's door.

How dare these unworthy creatures presume to control the divine prodigy, the wondrous phenomenon that was Maxwell Anderson. He whose feet mortal man was unworthy to kiss. He who was on Earth to represent the one true divine God. How dare they?

The people who had abducted Maxwell and his idiot father were clearly the spawn of the devil, intent on thwarting the Almighty's great will. The Boy-Giant had clearly been sent to this world to show humanity that not only was it God's will that everyone is different, Maxwell was also here to lead mankind out of the darkness of strife and conflict and into the light of peace and prosperity.

And what's more, many people had started to agree. His 'Worship Maxwell Anderson' Facebook page had over one thousand subscribers, and there were five hundred followers on his Twitter feed. He was the light and the way, and his followers would do his bidding.

But first, His followers had to release Him from the heathens who had dared to imprison Him in this ungodly incarceration. His followers must stand up and be counted for soon was the Day of Reckoning.

As the entrance rolled shut the man, furious and affronted, started to weep for the plight that the Chosen One was now enduring. His body was too big for the prison he was now captive in. His mind and soul, bigger still, would be suffering painfully. The man let out a scream of anguish, shaking his head vigorously, his long flaxen hair flying into his face, pink eyes aflame.

It was time to mobilise the Followers. Maxwell Anderson must be released unto the World.

The man reached for his smartphone, accessed his Twitter account, and began typing.

A call to arms.

61

THE TRUTH WILL SET YOU FREE

Swarthy, cadaverous and pony-tailed, Richard Crowe went about his work with quiet efficiency, and well-disguised glee. At last, a chance to test his theories, implement his discoveries and make his mark on the world.

It had been a smart move on his part to insist that Caroline equip the facility with a complete range of dinosaur toys and DVDs, an X-Box with all the latest games, and painting gear. With these trinkets and bribes, Crowe was able to befriend Maxwell quite easily. Most effective, however, was the presentation of a large cuddly Dalmatian toy, procured from a Disney superstore. Maxwell had immediately fallen in love with this, tears of sadness and joy flowing at the memory of his beloved Matthew. Crowe was especially proud of this piece of cunning; he and Max were now friends for life.

The first experiments, ostensibly at least, were about Max's personality, intelligence and aptitude, consisting of various psychological profiling techniques. At first these were conducted with Mark present, providing quiet reassurance to his son. As Max's confidence and ease around Crowe grew, Mark found himself a little superfluous. After two days,

Crowe managed to persuade Mark that it was scientifically necessary to continue the aptitude tests on Max without his father present, in case that Max's responses were in some way inhibited by his father's presence. Reluctantly, Mark remained in the living quarters, on standby in case required, and spent much of his time pacing the room.

Max was enjoying himself. He had Brackie and his dinosaur comrades. He had New Matthew to talk with, and cuddle at night. He had his X-Box. And best of all, his fantastic new friends Caroline and Richard. Richard was especially kind, and they played lots of fun games and quizzes. Max liked quizzes, he loved the chance to show off how brainy he was, and with Richard's quizzes he always seemed to get the answers right, which showed how clever he was. Christine would be proud of him.

Max had been carefully weighed and measured on his first day at Project Scorpio, and this became a daily routine. The measurements taken enabled bone density and body mass index to be calculated, and growth rate determined and predicted. Full body X-ray and CTI scans were taken, for which Max had to be sedated. He was frightened of the machinery, which had been adapted from an equine scanner in order to accommodate his extreme size, no doubt at extortionate cost, Mark had thought, as he consented to the sedative being administered. It also spared Max from the unpleasant dull ache of an X-ray beam, which Mark himself had always found excruciatingly uncomfortable on the few occasions he had had a suspected fracture.

Blood samples were also extracted when Max was sedated, which Crowe said would be used to assess whether

Max had the right mix of proteins and natural chemicals, and also to complete a DNA analysis.

This is all well and good, thought Mark, but he needed answers. What was causing Max's continued growth, as his height crept inexorably towards ten feet? What were the implications for his son's health? How would his physical needs be met? And most importantly, when would this ever stop? Getting answers to these questions was the sole reason for consenting to these Government experiments.

Mark was not able to give consent to the experiments that he did not know about, and was not asked his permission for.

62

LOST CAUSE

Late the next evening, under cover of darkness, the Followers began to gather in a hall on the outskirts of a village five miles from Project Scorpio. Squally rain and noisy blasts of cold air greeted the arrivals, many looking haggard, windswept and dishevelled after a difficult journey. The poor weather had at least kept many potential witnesses off the roads.

So as not to attract unwelcome attention, the hall had been booked in the name of an athletics club, having its Annual General Meeting. Two of the Leader's most trusted Followers, young men of about twenty-three, manned the door, access only possible with a covertly supplied password.

The Leader surveyed the assembled throng. The Chosen One's plight and the Leader's own exhortations had motivated a strong response, despite the short notice and remote location. He counted around eighty Followers standing about the hall, mostly young men and women, student-types who had latched onto a cause. He was seeing many of the Followers for the first time this evening, previously known only by an online pseudonym and avatar. Others he had met many times and there were silent nods of recognition as he looked around the room.

There was an agitated murmuring as the Followers awaited his address. Some chose not to interact, and waited patiently, alone amongst the multitude, quietly contemplating their thoughts. Dotted amongst the younger Followers were a few older people, one or two middle aged men in suits, a couple of pensioners, clearly more computer literate than most of their generation. The Leader noticed two teenage boys dressed in Scout uniform.

He suddenly felt a cold panic. He realised that he could not see the most important Followers of all – those who were absolutely pivotal to the success of the operation. Without whom not only were their endeavours doomed to failure – indeed, the whole enterprise would need to be abandoned – but more distressingly, the Chosen One would have to endure an extended life of incarceration, torture and servitude. Barely breathing and mind racing, he made for the exit, anxious that his Followers did not see his discomposure, and reached for his smartphone. Abruptly, two figures entered the hall at that moment, stopping the Leader in his tracks. A wave of relief flooded over him, as he first acknowledged the welcome presence of, Caroline Harris, manager of Project Scorpio, and Geoffrey Kelly, former physician to Maxwell Anderson. Now they were in business.

Dressed entirely in black, the imposing ensemble dominated by a three-quarter length leather jacket and thick, heavy boots, the Leader's albino skin and long white hair acquired an almost luminescent quality by contrast. He strode onto the wooden boards of the stage at the end of the hall, his thudding footsteps reverberating off the high ceiling. A hush came over the Followers, as they faced the stage, expectant, excited and apprehensive.

In fact, the detailed planning had been completed by an inner circle of the Leader and six senior Followers. The Seven, as they were known, had spent the evenings of the previous week ensconced at the Leader's home, working out all the steps needed to achieve their ultimate goal. Caroline Harris and Geoffrey Kelly belonged to the Seven and had been instrumental in determining the means to acquire the Chosen One, and designing the post-acquisition care. Twenty-four hours ago the plans had been distributed to the Followers through secure electronic media. Everyone gathered in the hall already knew their roles, but it was necessary for the Leader to look them all in the eyes, to ensure their absolute resolution, determination and loyalty to the Chosen One.

His composure returned and now breathing calmly, the Leader faced his Followers and began the speech that would irrevocably change their lives, and that of a certain ten feet tall boy, at that moment asleep at the Project Scorpio facility, cuddling his beloved artificial Dalmatian.

63

THE BUZZ

Twenty-thousand miles above their heads, a geostationary communications satellite, with superhuman efficiency and infinite patience, silently received the encrypted audio stream transmitted to it by one of the Followers.

An invisible speck in the vast blackness of space, the machine, a perfect combination of precisely engineered micro-electronics, computing power and solar energy conversion, relayed the signal to its human puppeteers on the surface below.

As sophisticated as it was, and despite being capable of processing many instructions simultaneously, the robot depended upon human intelligence to assess the relative risks and to confirm the decision to proceed with the operation as meticulously planned.

Unfeeling and opinion-less, the satellite beamed a signal to the Russian vessel riding the tumultuous swell of the angry North Sea.

The ship's master, a veteran of covert operations, surveyed the boisterous waves, icy rain stinging his face as the wind rammed the vessel with growing force. He allowed himself a short, violent curse as he read the tersely worded orders, issued by faceless administrators, their computerised weather map no match for an instinct in the ways of the sea that can only come from hard won experience, triumph and loss.

Mustering all the discipline and obedience of his lengthy and distinguished career, he pushed his misgivings to the back of his mind, and prepared to issue the necessary commands to his loyal, well-drilled crew. As the storm intensified, the master began to steel himself for the inevitable fatalities amongst his comrades.

The operation's success was paramount, naturally; and there could be nothing but an unswerving confidence that this would be achieved. Any losses sustained in the process were assessed by those in authority to be an acceptable price to pay, considering the huge advances in his country's scientific and military research that accomplishing the mission would bring.

64

SMOKE AND MIRRORS

Geoffrey Kelly listened to the Leader's exhortations, realising that the next few hours would probably be the defining moments of his life. Reflecting on the misery of his gambling addiction, which over the years had cost him his wife, career, friends and home, the nadir had been when he was caught shoplifting some basic groceries and a bottle of wine from his local mini-market store. He had got away with many previous thefts, targeting this store because their staff were typically dozy and intellectually challenged, he thought. Unfortunately for him, a new employee, a young woman, was more vigilant and soon rumbled his larceny. He now had a criminal record to add to a catalogue of life failures.

They're clever bastards, these gambling companies, Kelly had often rued. Every conceivable casino game, blackjack, poker, roulette, you name it, all available online, you didn't even need to leave your living room. Enticed by some 'free' money to get you started, and 'promises' of prizes of 'up to' many thousands of pounds, there was no reason not to have a go – as long as you only used the 'free' money, you couldn't lose. Registering a credit card and bank account was a mere formality, and how else could you receive your winnings? The early losses are just about outweighed by a few modest wins. However, the 'free' money is soon whittled down to a solitary virtual fiver and you think, what the hell, let's go out in a blaze of glory, and you have a punt on your favourite number on the roulette wheel – eighteen in Kelly's case – then, good grief, what are the odds? – eighteen is the number that comes up. Wow, what an adrenaline rush! The spine tingles as one hundred and eighty five pounds magically appears in the corner of the screen. Withdraw it now and you've beaten the system, the stupid fools running the website, they must be losing a fortune! And then flashing across the centre of the screen, big bright gold letters – "Play Again?" Well why not, it's still free money, there's no risk. And although the virtual money is soon depleted to zero, surely another roulette win will happen next time, it's the law of averages – it will cost only a fiver, or maybe ten, and then there's another ton-eighty! And so it had begun for Kelly and thousands of others, increasingly desperate as you spend more and more in a futile attempt to recoup past losses, surely another lucky win is a couple of mouse clicks away? You attempt ever more unlikely bets, accumulators and trifecta combinations, just need one of these to come off and you can then pay the electricity bill, or the TV Licence, or treat yourself to a bottle of wine – or as time goes on, keep the debt collector and his baseball bat out of the house for another week or so. But the lucky win never happens, the accumulator falls at the final hurdle, so with your last ten pounds you decide to play it safe, just bet on red, it's a fifty-fifty chance, surely you can't be that unlucky? And then a scream of frustration as the virtual ball lands on a virtual black number, you throw the mouse against the wall, it shatters into a thousand black shards and smashed circuitry, now you can't even use the computer to win your money back...

The evenings become a repetitive pattern of staring at the screen, occasional triumphs amongst regular despair. Evenings turn into long nights and you sleep barely three or four hours a night. You don't eat properly, don't have time to take care of household tasks such as laundry, you sometimes forget to wash and shave. Your colleagues and patients notice your dishevelled appearance but are too polite to mention it, until your supervising consultant takes you into his office and sympathetically but firmly makes clear that you look unprofessional and have body odour, complaints have been made about irritable behaviour and yawning during appointments. Only a verbal warning at this stage, but three strikes and you're out and things have got to change. You make an effort for a little while but before long the fatigue makes you late for work and you miss a few appointments, the appearance and personal freshness soon reverts to unacceptable standards. You are suspended and fail to turn up for your disciplinary interview, the hearing is conducted in absentia and just like that, your career is ended.

You turn to your friends for help, but although most are polite and say if anything comes up they'll think of you, others seem to give you every support short of help, and the phone never rings. You call people a second and third time but one by one people subtly or overtly make clear that you are persona non grata, and you are shunned and alone. One former colleague in particular, Richard Crowe, is quite unpleasant and even vindictive in his refusal to help his old friend. Two accomplices working together on the Maxwell Anderson case, trying to do good but in the process ensuring their own mark on the medical profession, and securing lucrative research contracts.

Embittered and angry by the rejection, Kelly had browsed the internet to catch up on young Maxwell, most of the tabloid publicity having passed him by. He came across what at first glance was a crank site, www.the-chosen-one-is-here.com, which contained an exhaustive archive of Maxwell Anderson press articles. Each one was accompanied by a lengthy diatribe exalting the status of The Chosen One as a young God amongst men who was being stifled and abused by his family, the authorities and the media. The site included a passionately written blog of preachings about the religious significance of a supernatural being in our midst, and how The Chosen One must be protected, a supreme entity amongst mortals, and a plea to sign up for Twitter updates. Kelly was not at all convinced by the alleged divine status of the baby he had helped to extract from his mother's womb, but it was curious that some people interpreted the superhuman growth as something godlike. Kelly had some insight into the medical reasons why a ten feet tall ten year old was on the planet, although even he struggled to explain why his and Crowe's ministrations had had such an unprecedented effect. Kelly had registered for updates, and engaged in lengthy email correspondence with the Leader, in which Kelly had explained his role with the Anderson family.

And now, his involvement complete and impossible to detach, he was embroiled in the Leader's crusade to rescue

Maxwell – The Chosen One – from the clutches of the evil Scorpio facility.

Although not without risk, this was his chance to recapture the glory, to be seen to be doing some good. It was a gamble, but the concept of weighing up the chances of success or failure was something he was all too painfully familiar with. He had concluded that he should not pass up the opportunity to renew his acquaintance with the Anderson family, possibly become their personal family physician, resurrect his lifeless career, pay for psychological counselling to finally kick the gambling, get his life back on track.

And in the process, there would be the incidental pleasure of exacting sweet revenge on Richard Crowe.

He listened to the Leader's vituperative incitements, joined the chorus of excited cheers and steeled himself for the operation ahead.

65

THE GLORY

The pituitary gland is a pea-sized object, located at the base of the brain. It performs many vital functions, surprisingly so considering its small size. The most crucial of these is the production and release of hormones that govern the growth rate of the body.

Doctor Richard Crowe had devoted much of his academic life and later career to the study of the pituitary gland and the bodily chemicals it synthesizes. As a child, he had been fascinated by the condition of his older brother, Adrian, who despite being a dwarf in the genuine medical sense of the word, led a normal life, as normal as possible anyway. There was teasing at school but Richard had stood up for his brother and was no slouch with his fists. The bullies soon learned to give them both a wide berth. However, when Richard was twelve and Adrian fourteen, beginning to feel the loneliness and sexual frustration of youth, Adrian had confessed his unhappiness at being different, and a desire to know what had made him like this. Adrian had turned to his younger but bigger brother for answers, which of course, at twelve years old, he had none. Richard resolved that one day, he would help his older brother.

By the time he encountered Mark and Melanie Anderson for the first time, Richard knew how to stimulate the pituitary gland to boost growth. When the scans showed the presence of an abnormally small but viable foetus, he had the perfect opportunity to test his theories and carry out his experimental treatment on a human subject, after years of tests on laboratory animals. Most of these tests had ended unsatisfactorily, with either no discernible results or startling gigantism, but Richard had told himself that was because he was not dealing with human DNA, and he had destroyed the test subjects.

And so it was, therefore, that the Anderson case provided a perfect opportunity – an ideal test subject for his pituitary stimulation experiments, and a second foetus which could be stealthily appropriated and sold without arousing suspicion. Showing the parents ultrasound photos from another woman's normal, single-foetus pregnancy was easy.

The actual birth, though, was unduly problematic as the second, larger foetus had grown to the extent that normal vaginal delivery was out of the question, and a regular Caesarean operation would have jeopardised the life of the smaller infant, due to the way the two babies' bodies were oriented inside the womb. There was no alternative but to cut away the abdomen in such a way that both babies could be lifted out together, prior to separation. Unfortunately, there was a minor detail in that there was no way the mother could survive such an emasculation, but the ends justified the means.

It had been straightforward getting the father, grief-stricken and not thinking clearly, to consent to a procedure intended to combat the unusual dwarfism in baby Maxwell. Crowe had performed the procedure on the infant's pituitary gland and watched and waited for the results.

What followed was beyond the expectations of Crowe, and he secretly panicked as Maxwell's amazing growth rate continued to the point of producing a genuine freak of nature. Attention was bound to be focused upon his own role in the development of young Maxwell, and his research would be exposed, and stopped. A way to counter the superhuman growth had to be found.

And now, at last, after several more years of painstaking research and illicit experimentation, Maxwell Anderson was back under the ministrations of Richard Crowe, and ready to undergo another prototypical treatment. Crowe looked down at Max, lying on his side, sleeping soundly, exhausted after a day of psychological tests and physical exercises, and oblivion ensured by a strong sedative that Crowe had covertly administered as Maxwell was preparing to take his toy Dalmatian to bed. He really is a titanic figure, Crowe thought, he had unleashed a brute upon the world. Tests showed that he was continuing to grow, and the rate was accelerating; he would reach an incredible twelve feet tall by his next birthday. There was no way to reverse growth, but it absolutely had to be stopped dead in its tracks.

Crowe reached down to Max's outsized head and gently lifted the unruly sandy hair at the back of his head so he could access the base of the brain. With the other hand he reached for his syringe, containing a cocktail of synthetic chemicals and natural genetic material, a formula effectively designed to put the pituitary gland into stasis, and cease the production of growth hormones. With as much care as twenty years' laboratory experience could muster, Crowe applied the syringe and delivered the potion. Max let out a troubled murmur as the needle went in, but remained asleep. The sedative was working.

Suddenly, Crowe heard two gunshots from elsewhere in the complex. The shattering noise echoed through the metal superstructure like the crack of a super-amplified snare drum in a concert arena. A terrible commotion of screams and shouting struck up. Cold dread flooded through Crowe's veins. What the bloody hell was going on?

66

THE END OF HOMELAND

Mark was on the phone to Julie when the Followers' attack on the Scorpio facility began. Distractingly, the wind howled and whined as it buffeted the Scorpio building.

Even without the acoustic interference, it had been a tense conversation. Separated by almost two weeks, they missed each other terribly, of course, but Julie had felt it necessary to spend these rare and precious moments together by berating Mark for failing to speak with her every day.

"I've been terribly worried about you, Mark. We all have," she had said.

"It's not been easy to find time to ring, babe." Mark always reverted to 'Babe' to try and placate Julie, to soothe a fraught exchange. "I've been very busy looking after Max."

"You're not in a bloody prison. You could have taken five minutes out, surely."

"But you're alright, though are you? Nothing bad has happened?"

"We're okay. Ralph is being a real trooper, stalling the press. They've got wind that something's happening. Your mum seems quite worried – there's someone else you've been neglecting."

"I'll call her tonight."

"Freddie called round today, to see how you are, and Max of course. I didn't know what to tell him."

"He's my oldest and best friend, we can trust him. Tell him the truth."

Julie paused. "He's still here now actually, he insisted on cooking us a meal. Keeping me company." That old rogue, thought Mark, he'd better not be getting any ideas.

"That was nice of him. Listen, Julie, I'm sorry I've not rung more often. I'll try to do better. I'm not sure how long we'll be here for. There are many more tests to be done and then they want to try some sort of treatment. But you're right, it's not a prison, and it should be possible for me and Max to take time out and speak to the people we love. And I do love you, babe."

"Aw, that's nice. I'm sorry for giving you a hard time. It's because I care about you – both of you."

"I know and that means everything to me. Look, Julie, when we get out of here, how about – WHAT THE HELL WAS THAT?"

Two deafening bangs shattered the rapport that Mark and Julie were just managing to establish. Yelling then filled the air, many voices, overlapping, drowning each other out, but evidently hostile, combative. Oh my God, thought Mark, MAX!

"What's going on, Mark?" implored Julie, but Mark had already dropped the phone. He dashed for the door connecting his room and Max's. He burst through, and recoiled with a jolt as he saw Crowe standing over a sleeping Max, syringe in his hand.

"Mr Anderson, I, er..."

"What in Christ's name are you doing? And what the fuck is going on?"

Outside, the shouting grew louder, and closer. Thunderous footsteps of many booted feet reverberated down the passageway.

Crowe, bewildered and faltering, just stood there gormless and hesitant. He looked fearfully towards the external door as a frightful pounding commenced, shaking the door in its frame.

Mark pushed Crowe out of the way and crouched down at Max's bed. He gave his son a shake, but he was sleeping soundly in spite of the bedlam that was exploding around them. Max emitted the low moan of a person enjoying a dream and not wishing to be wrenched away from it.

"Crowe, help me! Do something!" cried Mark as the noise outside grew more terrible, the hammering more thunderous now, reaching an ear-splitting volume. Three more gunshots pierced the tumult, and for an instant, a scream of pain drowned out the rest.

Mark felt nauseous, his stomach somersaulting and mind dizzy. Max was a dead weight, and would not be shifted. Crowe was a gibbering wreck. A feeling of utter helplessness descended over Mark, accompanied by a cold dread and a certainty that his son was about to be taken from him, probably be killed. The fact that he was likely to die in the process occurred as a brief afterthought and did not trouble him as much as the tragic fate about to befall his precious, beloved son.

Max, how I've failed you, Mark thought, as with a deafening crash the door burst open, and about a dozen disparate, frenzied invaders piled into the room with a raucous cheer. One member of the mob was silent and dignified among the chaos. Pale-skinned and white-haired, pink eyes burning like hot hail in the snow, he strode forward purposely toward Crowe and fixed him in a steely gaze. Crowe, transfixed, his eye sockets quivering slightly as he struggled to comprehend what was happening, was scared out of his wits. A dark wet patch began spreading down the front of his trousers. Without breaking the gaze, the Leader calmly raised a pistol, silencer fitted, and pressed it against Crowe's temple.

"Defiler and desecrator of all that is righteous, time to die," hissed the Leader, and pulled the trigger. A crimson geyser erupted from the back of Crowe's head, and he crumpled noiselessly to the floor, syringe still in hand. A pool of blood began to radiate across the floor.

The Leader raised his hands and in an instant the mob fell silent. "Followers, behold the Chosen One."

There was an eerie calm as the Followers patiently awaited the Leader's next words. In the background, a faint disembodied female voice, tinny on the smartphone speaker, cried out, "Mark! Mark!" Overcome by a maelstrom of violent emotions - terror, failure, helplessness, self-loathing and an incapacitating worry for his son, blackness enveloped Mark and he slid unconscious to the floor, his face coming to rest in the warm stickiness of Crowe's blood.

67

THE MAN'S GONE

"Mark! Mark!" screamed Julie into her phone, as Freddie rushed into the living room.

"What's going on, Jules?"

"I don't know! Something awful! I heard fighting, screaming, Mark's not answering, oh my God! Mark! Mark!"

"Let me hear." Freddie grabbed the phone and listened intently. "I can't hear anything. Marky, you there, buddy?" He turned to Julie. "Nothing. Oh hang on, here's something. "Some kind of chanting, I think – I can't make it out."

"Keep the line open!" demanded Julie as she lifted the landline's handset and pressed a button three times. "Police, quickly!"

Freddie regarded Julie's panicked anxiety, and felt a deep unease. Whatever was happening at the Scorpio facility was most definitely not part of the plan. Struggling to maintain his composure, he took out his smartphone and apprehensively began to place a call. The Comrade Colonel would be most displeased.

68

WHERE WILL I GO NOW

A familiar, metallic smell pervaded Mark's nostrils as he gradually regained consciousness. He was lying on a cold, hard surface. Confused and disoriented, as he tried to lift his head he became aware of a gummy substance connecting his face to the floor. Blinking, he tried to focus on the object nearest to him. It was a human face, a man's, strangely familiar. There was a coin-sized hole in the middle of the face's forehead, and a tentacle of dried blood curled down across the man's eye socket, nose and cheek.

Mark came to with a jolt, sudden realisation gripping him like a noose. The dead man was Richard Crowe, executed in cold blood by....who? Mark struggled to summon up the assassin's image. And why?

Max. They had come for Max. Panicking, abruptly awake, Mark sprang to his feet and dashed to his son's bed. It was occupied only by New Matthew, the large cuddly Dalmatian toy. "Max! MAX!" called out Mark, the only reply being a faint echo of his own voice. There was no-one else to be seen. Mark dashed out of the room into the main communication corridor. Lying about twenty feet from the doorway were two prostrate figures. One was wearing a laboratory coat, the other a security uniform fatigue. Both had been shot dead, blood spatter marks on the corridor walls.

"MAX!"

Still there was no reply. Mark made his way through to the main laboratory area and caught his breath as he surveyed the utter destruction before him. All the scientific equipment and computers had been smashed. The observation window, hidden behind a two-way mirror in Max's play area, had also been shattered, shards of glass strewn across the floor. Two more facility employees lay dead. Mark retched as nausea ravaged his body. He began to shiver.

Mark searched each area of the facility methodically but there was no trace of his son, just the violence and merciless murder inflicted by the invaders. Mark could now visualise the leader, a blond-haired man dressed all in black, including a leather trench coat. He made his way to the main entrance area and saw the spread-eagled corpses of two more security personnel, and as horrific as all this was, he was especially disturbed to see the body of the muscular, tight-suited agent who had first collected himself and Max from his home. There was no sign of Caroline Harris.

Mark bellowed out his son's name in despair and desperation. What the hell had happened here? Where had they taken his son? And why had he not been killed, like the others?

As his sub-conscious mind voiced these unanswered questions, he heard a number of vehicles approach at speed. Strobing electric blue light pierced the room. Thank God, he thought, surely the Police will know what to do? A figure stood in the entrance silhouetted by the neon blue.

"Please help me!" shouted Mark. Unexpectedly he felt a sharp needle pierce his chest. He looked down and saw that he was now affixed to what appeared to be an electric cable. Instantaneously after the realisation, the Taser charge ravaged his body, and oblivion took Mark once more.

69

THE STORM BEFORE THE CALM

Maxwell Anderson stirred uneasily from his sedative-induced sleep. It took him a few moments to locate the source of his discomfort. Feeling the back of his head, a throbbing, pulsing ache gnawed into his subconscious like a venomous wasp sting. He shortly became aware of an unpleasant, unfamiliar sensation of disorientation and nausea. He screwed up his eyes, wishing that the feeling would go away. With both arms he patted blindly around his bed, feeling for New Matthew the toy Dalmatian. Cuddling New Matthew would make Max feel better, it always did. When his hands touched nothing but warm, damp bedclothes, clammy from his own sweat, his eyes jolted awake and he tried to focus on his surroundings.

It was near dark, the only light coming from a dim source from outside the room, shining through an opening in the closed door. The room was small, just long enough to accommodate Max and his bedding which was lying directly on the floor; there was no bed. There was sufficient illumination for Max to see that the walls, floor and ceiling of the room were wooden. There was no other furniture.

As Max tried to get up, he was knocked off balance as the whole room abruptly lurched forward. Excited voices from outside the room struck up, people shouting at each other, frantic orders being yelled. The room rolled back in the opposite direction and Max's stomach somersaulted with it. He heard the loud crash of water and what sounded like the smashing of crockery. Suddenly Max realised – he was on a boat!

Fighting the urge to vomit, Max rose and cracked his head on the low wooden ceiling. Seeing stars, he crumpled back down to the bedding and began to sob. He called out for his Daddy. There was no response as the room tipped forward yet again, a deafening splash of water as another wave hit.

Head smarting from the lump now forming on his skull, Max half-crawled and half-stooped across to the door and looked though the opening. All he could see was the grimy grey wall of a ship's corridor, with shadows flickering from people to the right.

"Daddy?" Max cried out one more time, and again there was no response. Max tried the doorknob and was surprised to find that the door was unlocked and opened easily towards him. Barefoot and dressed in his custom-made Government-supplied blue pyjamas, he tentatively sneaked out of the room. The boat – or ship – Max was ignorant of what type of vessel this was, had clearly not been designed with ten feet tall people in mind! Almost bent double, Max turned right and shuffled towards the source of the shadows and commotion. Using his hands on each corridor wall to steady himself against the motion of the rolling ship, he slowly moved forward, calling "hello" as he did so.

An older boy, dressed in a scout uniform, ran up the corridor towards him, despatched on some errand. His gaze met Max's and both young men froze in their tracks. The scout stood still for a few seconds open mouthed with the shock and awe of coming into direct contact with The Chosen One. He turned around and scampered back down the corridor. Max could hear him calling "Help! The Chosen One is awake!"

Without warning there was another ear-splitting crash and the ship lurched heavily to Max's left. Max was young and completely uninitiated in the ways of the sea. However, one thing was clear: this was not normal. Something was badly wrong.

70

MY TIME OF DYING

The Leader silently seethed as he surveyed the scene unfolding before him. He cursed his luck. The meticulous plans determined by The Seven were in serious danger of being thwarted by this sea storm.

The operation at the Scorpio Facility had been straightforward. The loss of life was regrettable, but unavoidable. The heathens working for Scorpio must have known the risks when they decided to become enemies of The Chosen One. The actions of the Leader and the Followers were entirely justified in eliminating such enemies. Those who had died were casualties of war.

Caroline Harris had been upset, of course, several of her colleagues were now dead. Even though a certain amount of killing had been anticipated by The Seven, and rationalised as an acceptable consequence of freeing The Chosen One, the reality of it had been shocking to Caroline and she had frozen. Fortunately by this point, her key responsibilities had been discharged. The Followers had been guided into the facility and helped to locate the Chosen One. Caroline had been dragged away from Scorpio and onto the ship in an almost catatonic state.

Other than this, everything had gone smoothly. The Chosen One had remained asleep as the Followers gathered him up and transferred him to the minibus, seats removed and realigned to accommodate the prostrate and sacred body, ten feet long. The ninety minute journey to the Alexandra Docks at Grimsby had passed off without a hitch. It was a sensible precaution to escort the minibus with Range Rovers carrying armed Followers, but in the event this muscle was not required, as no-one sought to impede the Chosen One's progress. The Leader felt fortunate indeed that one of the Followers was the master of a merchant supply vessel. Such fortune was a sign that the Followers and their mission were meant to be.

Launching under a menacing sky, the ship had voyaged out into the North Sea en route to a destination known only to The Seven, the ship's master and its navigator. The choppy waters caused discomfort to many of the crew, The Chosen One, mawkish, snivelling and seasick, had been safely installed in his cabin, with Geoffrey Kelly assigned to monitor his condition and ensure that any medical needs were attended to.

Unfortunately, an unforeseen storm struck the ship about an hour out to sea. There were multiple possibilities, although it was pointless debating them: either the master had not checked the weather forecast, or had misinterpreted it. Alternatively, and this thought struck icy fear into the Leader's heart, the storm was a sign of displeasure from a divine source.

Either way, the ship was now in great peril. Huge forty-foot waves were now striking the vessel at frequent intervals, and the squally, cyclonic wind and murky visibility was preventing any sensible navigation. Most significantly, an engine failure was preventing the on-board pumping system from keeping ahead of the seawater that was inundating the ship and threatening disaster.

The master and various members of the ship's crew and Followers were rushing around and shouting at each other; the ship's discipline was breaking down. If the storm did not end quickly, they may be lost. The Leader's mind started racing. Sending a mayday call was out of the question, as The Chosen One was bound to be discovered. He would then be returned to the Scorpio facility, with strengthened security this time, to say nothing of the repercussions for the deaths of the facility's employees.

"Help! The Chosen One is awake!" It was the voice of one of the Scouts, who burst into the bridge. Kelly was conspicuous by his absence at the moment he is needed most, thought the Leader ruefully. Gracelessly, as the ship's rolling become ever more severe, the Leader moved into the corridor and faced The Chosen One, seeing him awake for the first time. Max's bulk filled the entire corridor, even doubled up as he was. The boy was terrified, bewildered, eyes pleading. Calling for his Daddy. It had clearly been a mistake to leave The Chosen One's father at the Scorpio building.

The ship suddenly rocked violently to the Leader's right, Max's left. They anxiously waited for the listing to stop and the ship to right itself. At the forty-five degree angle the tilting paused momentarily, and the Leader allowed himself a flicker of hope. An ominous rumble gave way to a cacophonous crash as a thousand items were ripped from their fittings and violently flung about the ship. Then, without further warning, the floor swiftly became the wall, and the ship gave up any last pretence of defying the elements.

The Leader was sobbing as the insatiable waters of the North Sea consumed him.

71

SOMETHING BLUE

MYSTERY OF BOY GIANT'S DISAPPEARANCE
By Mail Reporter, Ian Steele

Police and Government officials have refused to deny emerging reports that Maxwell Anderson, the tallest human being in history, has been kidnapped from the secret Government medical research facility in which he was believed to be staying.

Maxwell, 10, displayed an alarming rate of growth from a young age, had entered the Guinness Book of Records as the World's Tallest Person when his height reached nine feet last year. Currently believed to be over ten feet tall, Maxwell was until last night understood to be staying at a Lincolnshire science base, referred to in leaked documents as the 'Scorpio' project. His location is currently unknown following unconfirmed reports that armed terrorists stormed the Scorpio building and abducted Maxwell. A number of fatalities are thought to have occurred.

Speculation is growing that Maxwell may have been kidnapped for ransom, or taken by religious fanatics outraged at what they may perceive to be blasphemous and illegitimate treatment by the Government. Police were understood to be reviewing a number of websites and Twitter accounts for clues.

A Home Office spokesman said "There has been an incident at the Scorpio facility. Investigators are on the scene and it would not be appropriate to comment further until their work is complete."

Ralph Perkins, spokesman for the Anderson family, said that they had not heard from Maxwell or his father Mark Anderson since last night when a telephone call was abruptly terminated. Mr Perkins asked that the family's privacy be respected. He appealed for anyone with information to contact the security services.

Lincolnshire Police were today refusing to comment. However, there is every indication that a further cruel twist in the Maxwell Anderson saga may have occurred.

Do YOU have any information about the whereabouts of Maxwell Anderson or the incident at the Scorpio building? If so please contact the Mail news desk.

72

WHAT DO THEY KNOW?

Not for the first time, and nor would it be the last, Freddie hugged his best friend as Mark sobbed on his shoulders. It was now almost two years since Max's kidnapping. There was no sign of him, or a body, and Mark was clinging onto a faint hope that one day he would be reunited with his son.

In the immediate aftermath of the storming of the Scorpio building, Mark had to fight hard to demonstrate that he was not part of the operation, and was not at least indirectly connected with the murder of seven facility personnel and the disappearance of his son and the facility leader, Caroline Harris. Distressed and worried beyond reason about the fate of his son, Mark had had to endure insensitive interrogations and insulting innuendo by arrogant police officers who were presumably embarrassed at their own failure to anticipate the security risk Max posed.

It had taken several weeks for the police, working with MI5 internal security officers, to come up with a workable theory. Maxwell had been kidnapped by religious fanatics who had transported him to docks at Grimsby, and they had boarded a merchant ship, the *Hawley-Moore Belle*, which port records showed had sailed that evening. Radio contact and satellite telemetry had been lost a couple of hours after sailing, and the ship was presumed lost in the middle of the North Sea. RAF spotter planes had identified drifting debris and a slick of oil consistent with the foundering of a ship the size of the *Hawley-Moore Belle*. The debris had dispersed over a wide area by the time a Royal Naval vessel had arrived at the relevant coordinates, and no bodies were found. All aboard were presumed dead, including Caroline Harris, Geoffrey Kelly and Maxwell Anderson.

Mark refused to accept this and stuck to the belief that his son was alive, embarking on a crusade to convince others of this. A combination of almost evangelical campaigning to continue the search for Maxwell, together with pitiful self-loathing and guilt for failing to protect his son, had made Mark unpleasant and ultimately for Julie, unbearable. She left him almost six months after Maxwell's disappearance.

Ralph had been his usual genial reliable self and had ably dealt with the huge media interest in Maxwell's kidnapping, becoming the ubiquitous "spokesman for the Anderson family" in numerous newspaper articles and TV news reports. Inevitably, the interest died down with no new developments to keep the media's interest. With no Maxwell, there was no longer any commercial sponsorship or media fees, and Mark had to let Ralph go to pursue other opportunities.

Christine's was another painful departure, with no pupil to teach. Their parting was amicable and tearful.

For the first time in his adult life, Mark was alone.

Freddie had been a total rock and had moved Mark in with him once it became clear that his friend could not bear to be in the house that he shared with his beloved son and ex-girlfriend. There were too many painful memories. Despite the strain this put on Freddie's own life and relationships, he was unstinting in his support and hospitality for Mark who was clearly going through an excruciating turmoil. Many times though, he had patiently attempted to persuade his friend of the reality of Max's fate, drowned in the North Sea. At least Max was at peace, he told Mark, and would not now suffer the indignities and pain of a life blighted by abnormality.

There was simply no possible way for someone so conspicuous to be still alive and this not to be known to the authorities. Was there?

73

COLDER IN THE SUN

Franz Josef Land consists of almost two hundred ice-covered islands. It is the most northerly group of islands associated with Eurasia, at latitudes between eighty and eighty-two degrees, and around six hundred miles from the North Pole. With no indigenous population, the official recognised discovery of the islands was in 1873 by the Austro-Hungarian North Pole Expedition, who named the archipelago after the Austro-Hungarian Emperor Franz Joseph I. In 1926 the islands were taken over by the Soviet Union and a few people were settled there for research and military purposes. After the collapse of the Soviet Union, the islands became a territory of Russia, and despite frequent surveillance by western satellites, the exact nature of the operations at Franz Josef Land is unknown. It is known that a special permit and full military escort is required to visit the islands.

Zemlya Georga, or Prince George Land, is the largest island of the Franz Josef Land archipelago, with a distance of sixty-eight miles between its northernmost and southernmost ends. It was named by Benjamin Leigh Smith, a British yachtsman and explorer, after George, Prince of

Wales, who later became King George V. At the western end of Franz Josef Land, Zemlya Georga is a cold, inhospitable place, and access is difficult. It has a complex coastline, with many bays, deep inlets and capes. Most of the island lies under large glaciers, with only the peninsula at the northern end not permanently under ice.

Zemlya Georga provides perfect cover for clandestine shipping operations. In the early years of the Cold War, a marine base was painstakingly and laboriously carved into the glacial rock, a process that cost many lives of Soviet prisoners. Originally used to support nuclear submarines, by the turn of the twenty-first century its role had evolved to support surface vessels. The base is large enough to have one ship docked for maintenance and re-supply, while a sister vessel is active on espionage operations. The location enables ships to reach most parts of the Barents, Norwegian and North Seas.

The Russian spy ship *Pavel Podobin*, ostensibly an oceanographic research vessel, was three weeks out of Zemlya Georga and approximately ten miles away when the *Hawley-Moore Bell* got into difficulties in the middle of a severe cyclonic storm that few meteorologists had predicted. Fitted with stabilisers and accustomed as it was to navigating rough seas, nevertheless the captain and crew of the *Pavel Podobin* were tested to the absolute limits of their endurance and ability, and in some cases a little beyond; one especially large wave had swept two sailors overboard.

Throughout the storm, the Russian vessel tracked the British merchant ship by radar. When the storm was over, the radar operator alerted the captain to the disappearance of the main radar signal. The spy ship activated its more sophisticated scanning equipment, which soon revealed the existence of a debris field.

It took the *Pavel Podobin* almost forty minutes to reach the site of the stricken vessel and the debris field it had generated. With searchlights ablaze, the ship slowly pushed and nudged its way through patches of engine fuel, plastic bottles, food containers, unoccupied life jackets and general ship's detritus. A few dead bodies bobbed about in the water like children riding a swimming pool wave machine. After half an hour of searching, the Russian ship came across the *Hawley-Moore Belle*'s only two survivors.

Barely afloat and semi-conscious in a pathetically-small yellow dinghy, sharing the cramped space with the corpses of two drowned Followers, Caroline Harris weakly sounded her whistle and gesticulated at a patch of sea about twenty metres behind her.

The ship's powerful floodlights swept across to the area Caroline was directing. The captain, peering through binoculars, felt an exultant sense of triumph as he surveyed the brightly illuminated scene. Clutching the splintered wooden section of a cabin wall, suffering from hypothermia and frightened out of his wits, a huge but terrified ten year old boy was calling out for his daddy.

74

I WANT TO BE

Caroline's hypothermia had already progressed beyond the shivering stage as the *Pavel Podobin*'s crew plucked her from the dinghy. Disoriented, her mind and body were unable to respond to her rescuers' terse instructions. She was ungraciously draped across a burly sailor's shoulders, manhandled into the launch craft and roughly hoisted onto the main deck. She reeled unsteadily as though drunk, magnifying the motion of the ship. Her uncoordinated body was buffeted by strong gusts. Wind and spray stabbed her face, momentarily sharpening her senses. Her mind strained to focus but failed to penetrate the dense fog of confusion shrouding her brain. The ship lurched, and she tottered perilously close to the guardrail. Only the panther-like reflexes of a crew member, executing a successful dive and grab, prevented her from meeting oblivion in the unforgiving North Sea waters.

On the Master's orders, she was installed in the relative sanctuary of his cabin. Passive to the events around her, she submitted to her sodden clothes being stripped from her clammy skin. Roughly towelled and wearing dry, clean clothes, she finally succumbed to a crushing weight of fatigue. Her sleep was deep and dreamless.

*

Caroline slowly came to, emitting a low moan as the sea-worn hand of the ship's Master gently squeezed her shoulder.

"Miss Harris...Miss Harris..."

"Huh? Whassat? Whassup?" She tried to open her eyes and abruptly forced them shut against the piercing daylight. She became aware of a chilly air, despite being swaddled in the Master's spare bunk. A nourishing aroma of hot black coffee filled her nostrils. She gladly accepted the tin mug thrust into her hands.

"Miss Harris, you are safe aboard the *Pavel Podobin*. We are cruising northwards in calm conditions, and are perhaps sixteen hours out of Zemlya Georga."

Caroline snapped to reality as though slapped in the face. Thoughts flashed through her rapidly-awakening mind. Zemlya Georga. The *Pavel Podobin*. The terms had a strange familiarity, she recognised the words but could not comprehend their meaning. A spark of realisation, an ignition of memory. The shipwreck! The Leader! Project Scorpio! Maxwell Anderson!

"Oh my God! Maxwell Anderson! Is he on board? Is he all right? For God's sake, if we've lost him..."

"Do not be concerned, Miss Harris. The boy-giant was safely recovered from the wreck. We had been monitoring closely, and were ready to act when the decisive moment came. Everything is under control. You need not worry."

Caroline sensed an aloofness in the Master's manner towards her, like she was in some way unwelcome, or possibly mistrusted. She had many questions, and would not be deterred from asking them.

"But what about Maxwell? Is he harmed? How many others were saved? Tell me! You have a duty to cooperate, I'm the head of Project Scorpio!"

"You will receive a full debriefing at Zemlya Georga. My responsibility was to safely obtain the Anderson child and transport him to the facility. I have no obligations to you personally. You were rescued from the water on the specific instructions of my Government."

Caroline was calm despite the provocation; she could rationalise why the Master was being guarded towards her. The Project had had its mishaps; and most recently, the Followers and the storming of the Project Scorpio facility, although anticipated (and through Caroline's covert involvement, encouraged and nurtured), represented a highly variable factor which had huge potential to jeopardise the successful completion of the mission.

"At least tell me if he's hurt, for God's sake!"

The Master shrugged indifferently. "There are no serious injuries. He has some minor abrasions. He came aboard with hypothermia, much like yourself. He is currently sedated. I will ask the ship's surgeon to give you a full report."

"Thank you very much for your help, Captain," said Caroline, her words laced with irony, but he had already left the cabin. She wondered why the Master had bothered to wake her if he felt this inhospitable. Perhaps it was to make sure that her health was not deteriorating following the shock of the rescue. The Master would face repercussions if she suffered serious harm under his command.

The strategists who had devised the Scorpio Project, the first phase of the Tall Boy Project, knew that the requisite scientific expertise to create a viable subject only existed in

England. The political will and logistical capability to fully exploit the technology's potential was in Russia.

There were three vital elements to the Scorpio phase. Firstly to create a specimen that survived infancy. This had taken several attempts and gruesome failures. Secondly to ensure a stable environment for the specimen's development and study, while at the same time, managing the inevitable interest of the British Government. This had been Caroline's principal contribution, through working undercover in the Home Office and subtly influencing the powerful decision makers at Whitehall. The third phase was to effect a means of transporting the specimen to Russia without arising suspicion. Caroline was also instrumental in this, through infiltration and influencing the Followers. She had been the instigator of the plan to stage an assault on the Scorpio building and spirit Maxwell away by sea.

The *Pavel Podobin* had been deployed essentially as a pirate ship, to hijack the *Hawley-Moore Belle* and see it safely delivered at Zemlya Georga. The storm and the inept seamanship of the Followers combined to turn this into a rescue mission and salvage operation. The difficulty and risks for the Master of the Russian vessel had increased exponentially without possibility of proper preparation. This is probably why he was so offhand with me, thought Caroline.

She was able to reflect, though, that if Maxwell Anderson was reasonably unharmed, as the Master had indicated, she had discharged her responsibilities well. Assuming the name Caroline Harris when beginning her undercover assignment as a sociology student in England all those years ago, her birth name of Valentina Rykov was known only to her superiors in Moscow. Arrival at Zemlya Georga would see the successful completion of the Scorpio phase of the Tall Boy project. She hoped that her next assignment would be equally as challenging and rewarding, although ideally, she would prefer one of shorter duration.

Her nagging doubt was that despite taking steps to silence the odious reporter Johnny Bird, at some point there was an extra dimension to the Maxwell Anderson story that would demand decisive action.

75

SUPERNATURAL

The injection Richard Crowe administered to the base of Maxwell's skull, minutes before the storming of the Scorpio building by the Leader and his Followers, did not have the effect that the duplicitous doctor desired. Crowe, shot through the head by the Leader himself, would never see the consequences of his final failure, for which he paid the ultimate price.

The cocktail of synthetic chemicals and genetically modified proteins was designed to immediately halt Maxwell's continuing enlargement. This would be achieved by neutralising the hormones in Maxwell's pituitary gland, and leaving in place artificial inhibitors that would prevent any attempt by Maxwell's body to regenerate its natural capacity for growth.

In fact, during a process that unfolded in front of the team of Russian anthropologists to whom Maxwell had been assigned, the precise opposite effect occurred to the one Crowe expected. Seemingly stimulated into overdrive by the needle's assault and the serum's infiltration, Max's pituitary gland throbbed into life and emitted a new torrent of endorphins and pheromones which pulsed through his body with irresistible force.

The effect, which alarmed, fascinated and thrilled the scientists in equal measure, was a spurt of growth unprecedented even in Maxwell's life. Ten years old and a little over ten feet tall when recovered from the North Sea, his height expansion was measured at almost an inch per week. By Maxwell's eleventh birthday, he had reached a scarcely comprehensible thirteen feet seven inches tall.

Many of the practical difficulties experienced by Maxwell in former days soon re-presented themselves. Clothes and shoes were of course impossible to source from regular outlets but once specially constructed items were provided (their manufacturers sworn to secrecy, and informed that indiscretion would be met with dire retribution), they were soon rendered useless and had to be replaced at significant cost. Doorframes began to be hazardous obstacles again, and Maxwell reverted to wearing head protection, a hard plastic skull cap which would be more easily replaced with larger versions than a full helmet. Every boy who is approaching puberty has a voracious appetite, but one growing at Maxwell's rate was insatiable. Although his carers were, in general, fond of him, his incessant whining and complaining of hunger often tested the patience, not to mention the skill and ingenuity of the resident caterer. Bathroom facilities again became problematic and was the source of much upset and humiliation to Maxwell due to frequent accidents.

Emotionally, Maxwell was found to be well-adjusted albeit traumatised by the *Hawley-Moore Belle* shipwreck and the apparent loss of his father. He had a natural reserve and shyness, a consequence of having little social contact in his life. Maxwell, having endured more turmoil than most children, was adjudged by psychologists to be a resilient boy with a phlegmatic attitude to life. He bonded well with his new scrutinisers, and became a special friend of a pretty young nurse called Olga. His passion for painting returned, zoo animals and Dalmatians being his most common subjects.

A foreseeable and yet somehow unforeseen set of new difficulties began to emerge, at first gradually, and then with worrying, snowballing acceleration.

The human skeletal system is a miraculous feat of natural genetic engineering, refined and enhanced through countless generations of evolutionary development. Bones are versatile, ingenious and strong. They support the body, indeed, prevent it from rolling about on the floor like some overgrown amorphous amoeba. Bones protect vital organs, facilitate fluidity of movement and enable the senses to work. They are essential to a healthy existence.

However, no man-made construction or machine would perform reliably at over double its intended design specifications and so it is with natural structures too. The skeleton has been carefully developed to operate effectively in a human being with an average height of anything between five and seven feet tall, with a degree of latitude at either end of that range. To expect a complex framework of over two hundred interlocking, moving parts to work well at twice their intended size is unrealistic. Like a skyscraper built too heavy for its steel girders, stresses and strains will appear, imperceptible at first, but steadily worsening until malfunction and even a catastrophic collapse is possible, and perhaps inevitable.

And so it began to transpire with Maxwell. A subtle and for him, indescribable inability to get comfortable while sitting or lying down was the first sign of more serious problems to come. As this turned into a tearful chronic insomnia, his Russian keepers resorted to using sedatives while proper diagnoses were performed. This was hampered by the lack of MRI and other scanning equipment able to accommodate Maxwell's gargantuan size.

It was relatively straightforward to confirm the early onset of osteoarthritis in Maxwell's feet, ankles, knees and hip joints; this was certainly the most likely explanation for the sharp, burning sensations he was starting to experience.

The stiffness and constant, debilitating pain in Maxwell's spine, gnawing away at him like a vampire leech, was more challenging; numerous theories abounded. When his eyes became raw, sore and painfully insensitive to bright light, the doctors determined that ankylosing spondylitis, a form of chronic, inflammatory arthritis, was, tragically, the condition that was now plaguing Maxwell's young life. The doctors considered it kinder not to reveal to Maxwell that he would be beset by persistent pain spreading throughout most of his body for the rest of his life, with a rigid, fused spine and disabling immobility almost certain to blight his existence at some point in the not too distant future.

The doctors speculated that as Maxwell's growth continued, so his bones would increasingly struggle to cope with the massive load being placed upon them. They simply would not develop the density and strength in the proportion necessary to keep pace with the other changes in his body. They would become brittle and fractures were almost certainly going to be frequent occurrences. As the osteoporosis intensified in the coming years, Maxwell's posture would become hunched, and his sense of balance would erode away until falls became commonplace. The result would be a vicious cycle of more broken bones, pain and misery.

Olga followed these medical developments with an anguish that grew to consume her whole being, like an aggressive tumour. She was careful to be brave, strong and cheerful while with Maxwell himself. She was a huge source of comfort to him during the many extensive medical tests he was subjected to, a stabilising oasis of calm and positivity in a maelstrom of bewilderment and pain. As much as she enjoyed being with Max and helping him through these ordeals, she began to long for the nights to arrive, granting her the succour of solitude and the opportunity to let her efficient Russian veneer slip away. Sobbing herself to sleep became routine. Osteoarthritis, osteoporosis and ankylosing spondylitis was a tragic cocktail of agony for anyone to endure, but she was heartbroken that a sweet young boy such as Maxwell should fall victim to it. And who knew what other ailments would strike as his tallness continued to reach unprecedented heights? While her colleagues became fascinated by Maxwell's medical curiosities Olga shuddered to think what the future may hold for him.

There were those amongst the Russian intelligentsia who argued that the ethical and humane thing to do was to return Maxwell to his country of birth and his family. On pragmatic economic grounds, studying and caring for Maxwell was a significant expense with questionable benefit for Russia. Few scientific insights could be derived from a unique and unprecedented case, which in all probability would not ever reoccur, and experiments so far had failed to replicate the phenomenon. It was better for Russia and for Maxwell himself to let him go.

On the other side of the argument were the hardliners, concerned about the damage to Russia's interests if it was revealed to the world that not only had covert operations been taking place in the North Sea, a British citizen had effectively been kidnapped, and information of use to the investigating authorities in England had been withheld. Furthermore, the fact that a young boy had been incarcerated in a Russian institution would not play out well in the world's media. They were adamant that the whole basis for initiating the Tall Boy project – on which all the plans had been founded, and painstakingly implemented, the funding of illicit science, the recruitment of British agents – was still valid. It was undoubtedly the case that there was scientific value in Maxwell, it was just a matter of time until Russian scientists could discover the key elements and seek to reproduce it for Russian technology to develop, to the benefit of medical science, and possibly, for military use. A Russian brigade of giant super-soldiers could have distinct advantages – although, as a subversive comrade had pointed out, they would be bigger targets.

The matter was escalated to Russia's president. A more conciliatory figure than some of his predecessors, the President was implementing a programme of domestic social reform and a repositioning of foreign policy, both of which were designed to project the image of a stable and prosperous trading partner with humanitarian values and a nation capable of playing a pivotal role in the resolution of international crises. In short, the President was trying to displace the United States as the world's go-to superpower.

The President, and his advisers, calculated that a certain course of action would deliver maximum advantage to their homeland. It was characteristically courageous and not without risk.

Maxwell Anderson celebrated his twelfth birthday as a fluent Russian speaker, accomplished artist, above-average chess player, and a little over fifteen feet tall. His existence was about to be revealed to the world.

76

MOTHER

Olga Metovsky was the daughter of a decorated Red Navy submarine commander and a primary schoolteacher. She had inherited her father's red hair, cunning and capacity for hard work, and her mother's asthma, love of Beethoven and ability to establish empathy with children. A bright student, displaying an early interest in diverse subjects such as Russian history, music, architecture and English literature, Olga decided at the age of sixteen that psychology would be her primary focus in life, inspired after reading a book by Aleksey Leontyev. Through connections her father was able to make, an internship in a military hospital was procured, with her mother able to broker a place at a top university to enable Olga to match the theory to the practice. Now recently graduated, Olga's talent was spotted by a Government scout and she was installed as a nurse in a state psychological facility. She developed a talent for treating post-traumatic stress disorder, easing the suffering of shell-shocked veterans of covert military operations. A secondment to the Tall Boy Project was a logical step, and chance for Olga to make an indelible mark in the minds of extremely important people. Looking a good few years younger than her actual twenty-four years, her freckly complexion and beaming smile were ideal attributes to charm her superiors and Maxwell Anderson alike.

Olga had been an ever-present factor in Max's life since he was rescued from the North Sea, brought back to Zemlya Georga, and spirited to a safe house close to the town of Rostov, two hundred kilometres northeast of Moscow. The safe house was actually a disused monastery, for the last couple of decades or so operating as a training hospital and research facility. Its cavernous chambers and inaccessibility could not have been more suitable for the Tall Boy project.

Before meeting Max, Olga was instructed in her role, in essence to be his friend, to help him acclimatise to his new home and come to terms with not seeing his family, and to perform discreet psychological evaluations. She carried out all of these duties diligently and effectively.

Her first encounter with the frightened ten year old, then still only a little over ten feet tall, almost derailed their relationship before it began. It was one thing having someone tell her what to expect and quite another to come into direct contact with such an extremely unusual human being. Her initial reaction, upon meeting someone so tall up close and personal, was to recoil in slight horror and amazement at the sheer enormity of the boy. Wide-eyed and hand instinctively over her mouth to stifle a small scream, she was sure that Max picked up on her negative body language. Initial feelings of shock and awe were immediately replaced by sympathy at the cruel aberration that nature had inflicted on a young boy. Tears had welled in her eyes. Olga came to learn that Max was used to seeing people react in this way, and had become inured to any offence or awkwardness such behaviour would otherwise cause. Within a few minutes of meeting Max, Olga's psychology training kicked in, she reminded herself firmly that here was a human being with feelings, separated from home and family and in all probability bewildered and terrified. She stood on a chair, held out her arms and hugged young Maxwell as tightly as she could, whispering soothing noises into his ear. Max would always remember this gesture of unconditional kindness, and in the months and years to come would eagerly anticipate Olga's presence, and be morose when she was not around.

For Olga's part, after two years of caring for and working with Max, and seeing his physical and emotional development at first hand, she was as much in love with him as any mother is with their son. She simply could not bear the thought of any harm coming to him.

It had been an otherwise routine day for Olga and Max when she became aware of some unusual activity. A visitation of several unfamiliar Government officials, after briefly observing her interactions with Max, ensconced themselves in the office of her commanding officer. Comrade Colonel Alexsandr Parov was a brusque, lecherous man whom Olga did her best to have as little to do with as possible. Her curiosity about what has happening in Colonel Parov's office mushroomed into bewilderment when he telephoned Max's day room and tersely ordered her to have Maxwell ready to go on a journey in one hour.

With Colonel Parov's words still ringing in her ears, and no small sense of dread over what was to occur, she entered Max's living quarters, built into a converted monks' dormitory, ceiling removed and custom-sized furniture and utilities installed with the manufacturers sworn to the same secrecy as those who made Max's clothes. He was sitting cross-legged on the floor, staring with a puzzled expression at a large plasma screen mounted high on the wall. A game of computer chess was displayed, and Max was calculating the likely consequences of a few possible moves. The sandstone walls were adorned with many of Max's paintings; a few each of Brackie and Matthew, and Olga herself featured on a couple of portraits. However, one design in particular dominated the room. Repeated many times, variants on the same theme: two people, side by side and holding hands, walking towards a brilliant orange sun. The figure on the right was typically twice the height and double the width of his companion: He was looking back over his shoulder, fixing the picture's viewer with a mournful gaze, a tear on his cheek. Olga's compassion for a boy missing his father swelled every time she saw them.

"Max, dearest, we're going on a trip. Have you nearly finished your game, my sweet? We need to get ready."

Max looked across at Olga and smiled. She took a moment to marvel at the sheer size of the twelve year old. It was a sight she felt she could never get used to. It was a fascination to her that Max's body had kept in relative proportion with itself, in stark contrast to people with less extreme height disorders. Now three times the height of an average adult male, Max's head alone was the size of a beach ball. His blond hair and hazel eyes gave him a pleasant appearance, it would be a shame when the inevitable teenage spots ravaged his complexion in the next few years. She was forgetting for a moment that the prospect of Max being able to enjoy a normal loving and physical relationship was quite remote.

"Where are we going?" he asked.

"To a television studio. Come on, I'll help you have a wash and put your best things on. We're going to be on the news."

77

SOMBER DAYS

Two thousand miles away, Mark Anderson was in his living room, sat uncomfortably at his PC. It was set up on a self-assembly unit with sliding keyboard shelf, PC unit and printer underneath, cunningly designed so that you could not get your legs in and hence the unit was as ergonomically unsuitable as possible. The radio was on, a one-day cricket match between England and India. England were losing.

Unshaven and in unwashed t-shirt and jogging bottoms, Mark was busy surfing through job vacancy websites, a daily process for him now, as he needed an income. Monies made through the opportunities created by Ralph Perkins were now all but exhausted. Two years after Max's disappearance, the media were no longer interested in him, plenty of new emergencies and human interest stories to fascinate tabloid readers and shock-doc viewers.

A few times in recent months he had had to swallow his pride and ask for handouts from his parents and also from Freddie. Roger, mourning his grandson as deeply as Mark was struggling to come to terms with the loss of his son, was coldly unsympathetic, telling Mark in no uncertain terms that it was long overdue for him to pull his life together and get a proper career back together. At forty-five, time was running out for Mark, Roger had said. In characteristic fashion, Shirley proved to be a softer target, and was able to make a small amount of cash available, and always sent Mark away laden with food supplies. Freddie, ever the affluent playboy and loyal friend, had given Mark a few thousand pounds, but Mark was now sensing a reluctance on Freddie's part to socialise or even speak on the phone, and a few recent emails had gone unanswered. Presumably Freddie was wary of being asked for further handouts; apart from the financial aspect, such things can ruin friendships.

Mark exhausted the usual local agency sites and moved onto the national pages, starting with the Guardian. Vacancies advertised here were usually out of his league, but you never know. Abruptly his concentration was broken by an excitable "BOWLED HIM!" on the radio, England losing another decisive wicket. Useless bastards, Mark thought, as the multitude of Indian fans began screaming adulation for their heroes, drowning out the commentary.

Distracted from the key task at hand, Mark went to the kitchen to get a drink. The telephone rang, an increasingly rare occurrence these days. Sprinting back to the radio, he hit the off switch and grabbed the receiver.

"Hello?" he answered, uncertainly.

"Mark, it's Julie," came the reply. Mark stared in amazement at the 'phone. This was the last voice he was expecting to hear, although he had so often craved to hear from his former fiancée since their traumatic parting eighteen months ago. Why was she suddenly calling now, after all this time? A flicker of hope fizzed through his brain. She had kept his number!

"Hi Julie, what..."

She cut him off. "Mark, listen. You have to put the TV on. BBC1. NOW!"

"Sorry, what? The TV? What's going on?"

"Just DO IT!"

78

THE EYES OF THE WORLD

Mark grappled clumsily with the plasma's power cable and eventually coaxed it into the socket. He switched on the set and waited impatiently while the agonizing fifteen seconds it inexplicably took to warm up and allow the right channel to be selected.

"Come on, you bloody thing!"

The first thing he noticed was the "BREAKING NEWS" banner emblazoned across the bottom of the picture. Scrolling maddeningly slowly underneath were the words "Maxwell Anderson, world's tallest person, found alive in Russia".

Confused, Mark saw that a grey-suited man was stood at a podium behind which the white, blue and red stripes of the Russian national flag were affixed to the wall. The man was speaking in Russian, his voice mixed low in the audio track to allow for the monosyllabic tones of the BBC's translator, who was female, rather confusingly. Mark listened intently.

"...best of care in a secure facility close to Moscow. Maxwell is a happy and healthy boy. His carers have become extremely fond of him. However, like any young man, he cannot stay in one place forever. The next stage in his emotional and intellectual development is to allow him freedom of choice and freedom of movement."

The spokesman paused, looked up directly to the camera and gulped, almost imperceptibly. Mark's mind was a blur. What's going on? Max alive? How? In Russia? Where? Is he well? Is he still growing? What's been going on all this time? Why haven't I been told? All these questions and a thousand more fizzed through his brain at the speed of light.

The man started speaking again, followed by the interpreter a few seconds later. "The Russian Government appreciates that the revelation of Maxwell Anderson being alive will be shocking to many people. The fact of his rescue from the North Sea accident being withheld from the British Government and his own family, we recognise will be of similar surprise and concern."

"Too bloody right," Mark hissed at the screen. His telephone began ringing, but he ignored it.

"We believe that at all times we have acted in the best interests of Maxwell. He came to our nation as an emotionally damaged boy, overwhelmed with stress. Our finest experts concluded that an extended period of stability was essential for his long term welfare. The Russian nation is caring and compassionate and has humanitarian values at its heart. Sometimes the needs of one person outweigh the needs of many."

Mark's mind briefly flashed back to his appalling meeting with Mrs Taylor, the Headteacher who expelled Maxwell from school. She had used the opposite argument to justify her cruelty.

"WHERE'S MY SON?" he yelled at the screen.

"The Russian Government recognises that there will be

many people who feel that we did not handle this in the right way. We acknowledge that some Western governments are likely to feel that Russia has behaved poorly. While we would not agree with such an assessment, we respect other points of view. To anyone who is unhappy with what we have done, we say that we are sorry. The Russian Government is keen to adopt a more conciliatory approach to foreign policy and we trust that our actions today demonstrate goodwill."

The spokesman paused again, as if milking the spotlight, clearly conscious that his words were being heard by many millions around the world. Again, he spoke, with the same short delay before the incongruous female translation.

"People of the world, here is Maxwell Anderson, the tallest human being in history."

He stepped away from the podium and the camera panned back. Emerging from the right of the stage was a young red-haired woman, dressed primly in black jacket and trousers. Her left arm was held high above her head, and as the camera panned back further, it could be seen that her hand was being held by an enormous fist. Immediately behind the woman was a moving column of black fabric, festooned with what appeared to be metalwork attachments, as Mark realised with horror that this woman came up to a point just above Max's knee. Still the camera panned backwards and now Max's torso was in shot. Mark let out a choked half-laugh, half-cry, as he noticed that Max was wearing a jersey emblazoned with a recent movie poster version of a brachiosaur. Overwhelmingly, Mark's thoughts turned to apprehension as the enormity of what Max had become began to unfold – in front of millions of people – that his son, the tiny, pathetic baby he had once cradled in his hands, was now absolutely gigantic, a monster amongst men.

He shuffled painfully across the studio floor. Hunched over like a frail old lady; even stooped, his blond hair scraped the ceiling; it was buzzcut short, the tousled blond mop of the young Maxwell was no more. He wore thick wraparound sunglasses, jet black, mercifully concealing the pain and bewilderment in his eyes. With one hand engulfing Olga's, the other hand tightly clasped on a caber-like walking stick. Mark let out a small whimper of anguish as he saw that Max wore leg braces, his young bones and muscles no longer able to carry his enormous weight.

Mark focused on Max's face, trying hard to recognise the person that was his son. The sunglasses dominated Max's features, rendering it impossible to fully discern his emotional state. Mark searched for signs of happiness and contentment, but all he could feel from the screen was anxiousness. That poor boy, he thought, how dare they parade him in front of the media without his father there to look after him?

The red-haired woman looked up at Max and gave him a supportive smile. The BBC anchor-man, with ubiquitous baritone Welsh accent, spoke about "extraordinary scenes" as Max, radio microphone pinned to his jersey, looked down the camera lens. The world held its breath as Maxwell Anderson, presumed dead in a failed kidnap attempt and shipping disaster, prepared to utter his first words.

Barely audible, timid and faltering, Max said, "I want my Daddy," and Mark sobbed.

79

THE WAY HOME

Despite the collective might of the Russian logistical machine, transporting a fifteen-foot tall human being from Moscow to England was not an easy task to accomplish. No civil or commercial aircraft was designed for such a purpose. In an experience that made Max think grimly back to his journey in the back of a Government van to the Scorpio building, he found himself lying down, lightly strapped onto a makeshift trolley-bed, and wheeled into the cargo hold of a military transport plane.

Colonel Parov allowed Olga to accompany Max on the journey home. This had not been his original intention and it was not an uncharacteristic show of compassion on his part. He had turned down Olga's original request, and was subsequently unmoved by her passionate beseeching immediately after the press conference. With a lascivious grin and sledgehammer innuendo, he made clear that he was open to persuasion. Accepting the gruesome reality of her situation, Olga finally resorted to fellatio to convince the unpleasant Parov of the need to display some humanity. He made clear that similar favours of her would be expected when she returned.

Olga was distraught at the prospect of her parting from Max. After two years of working with him, she had come to feel awe, wonder and pity at his appalling condition. She was desperately worried about what would become of him without her to care for his needs. Overriding all of that, however, was the fact that Max was a likeable boy whom she had formed a special bond. She enjoyed his company and would miss this terribly. Despite the emotional conditioning of her upbringing, she loved Max, and wanted to be with him. Tragically for them both, she thought, this was being cruelly denied.

Three days after the press conference, the plane took off and headed to its destination, ironically and tactlessly, the Lincolnshire airfield where the Scorpio facility had been situated. This had long since been dismantled, the only trace was now a gravestone-sized memorial stone that honoured the Government employees who died in Max's kidnap. An advance entourage had set off an hour previously, assorted officials and diplomats, and a high ranking representative from the Russian foreign ministry.

Olga was with Max, her hand clamped around his thumb, itself the diameter of her wrist. Competing with the shuddering rattle of the plane in flight – it was not built to facilitate easy conversation – she prattled to him about their experiences together, chess games played, his Russian language lessons. Max was distracted, uncommunicative. What must this poor boy be going through she thought, and blinked back tears, determined that his final memory of her would not be one of weakness and sadness.

With a judder and convulsion that made Olga's heart and stomach swap places, the plane completed its final banking manoeuvre and began its gradual descent to the English countryside. She steeled herself for their final moments together.

Max was going home.

80

REUNION

It was late afternoon, British time, as Mark peered high into the Eastern sky, keen to get an early glimpse of Max's plane. The advance party had arrived over an hour ago, and Russian officials were now mingling awkwardly with their British counterparts. Mark looked smarter than he had for a long time. Shaved, showered and dressed smartly, he wanted Max to be proud of his father. His mind was a whirlwind of disbelief at what was happening, coupled with anger at the Russian authorities for depriving him and Max of two years of father-son bonding. At the same time Mark was elated that first and foremost, his son was alive! However, any hope he felt about his and Max's life together was tempered by a nagging dread that quite clearly, the abnormal growth had accelerated to a point where any prospect of a remotely manageable life was fast disappearing – literally, skywards.

His parents, Roger and Shirley, had accompanied Mark to the airfield, a gesture which he greatly appreciated. Despite the bluff exterior, his father was clearly fond of his grandson – and, Mark liked to think, the experiences of the last twelve years or so had brought them all closer together. The real thrill however was that Julie was also with him on this crucial day. Within a couple of hours of the press conference, she was in his living room, and hugged Mark tightly as a maelstrom of emotion cascaded out of them both. Julie had been devastated by Max's disappearance and his assumed death. An intense hope of Mark's during this past three days, which he dared not say out loud in case he jinxed the possibility, was that the mutual joy they felt upon being reunited with Max would rekindle their relationship. Getting Julie back into his life – and, he very much hoped, his bed – was something Mark did not think was possible only three days ago.

They all had a sense of being watched. Government security had prevented any media people from coming onto the airfield, a necessary measure to avoid an emotionally-charged event becoming unbearable, especially for Max. However, although from their position they could not be seen, a phalanx of photographers and cameramen, all equipped with state of the art zoom lenses, encircled the site, like zombies at a shopping mall, ready to capture whatever images they could of the tallest human being in history. Maxwell Anderson was big news once again; Mark had urgent need of the services of Ralph Perkins once more. Ralph had been only too delighted to be re-engaged.

"There it is!" exclaimed Roger, pointing at the sky. It took Mark a few seconds to focus, as the clear shape of an aircraft materialised out of the clouds. As it neared the landing strip, Mark saw that it resembled a Hercules, but somewhat squarer and apparently less aerodynamic, causing him to wonder how on Earth the thing was able to stay in the air. His heart leapt into this mouth as the plane visibly wobbled on the approach, the pilot seemingly fighting to keep his machine horizontal and aligned with the runway. For God's sake, don't crash now, thought Mark. With an ungraceful thump and screech, the plane kissed the tarmac and trundled to an undignified halt.

Julie held Mark's hand but it was Roger who surprised the most. He put a fatherly arm around Mark's shoulder and squeezed hard.

"This is it, son," he said, with moistened eyes. "Be brave for the lad."

Several officials stood patiently at the rear of the plane as the cargo door slowly hissed open. Mark and his companions craned their necks, desperate to glimpse the plane's innards and hopefully, Max. This was nerve-wracking for Mark. Is Max healthy? How has his personality been affected by two years separated from his family, imprisoned in a Russian institution? Will he forgive his father for abandoning him? Will Max even recognise or acknowledge his family? How the hell are they going to cope with a fifteen foot tall human being, with all the emotional needs and frailties of any pubescent child, magnified a thousand-fold?

Pleasantries and formalities between the dignitaries having been completed, officials fanned backwards to clear a route for Max to leave the plane. With several burly men in combat fatigues bearing the strain, Max, still strapped to his trolley, was slowly wheeled down the ramp, head first, unable to see his family just yet. A red-haired woman walked sombrely behind, whom Mark recognised as Max's companion from the Russian press conference. Shirley let out a whimper as the enormity of Max's shape became apparent, but also the fact that he was struggling against his restraints.

"Oh, that poor boy," she sobbed.

Mark could contain himself no longer. Breaking free from Roger and Julie, he sprinted over to the trolley and pushed aside the officials and soldiers milling around his son. He looked into Max's eyes – sunglasses removed for the darkened plane interior – and was relieved to see an affectionate recognition spread across his face.

"Hello Daddy," Max said.

"I'm here, Max, I'm here." Mark frantically struggled with the buckles. "For Christ's sake, someone help me get him out of this!"

After a few frenzied seconds, finally the strapping was removed. Max uncurled his gigantic limbs and he rose unsteadily, planting his enormous feet on English soil for the first time in over two years. Mark looked up at his son, pleadingly, imploring, desperately searching for some sign of affection and forgiveness.

Dismayed, Mark saw Max look through him and directly to the redhead, waiting a discreet distance behind. Max lumbered across and scooped her up in his arms. They were both weeping and exchanging impassioned words in Russian. It was abruptly clear to Mark how important this person had been to his son during his time away. Max's return to his family was clearly coming at considerable personal cost: the severing of a bond.

Mark approached the pair as Max gently set her down on the ground. She turned to Mark and proffered her hand.

"I'm Olga, Mr Anderson," she said, wiping away tears with her other hand, "you have a wonderful son. Please take good care of him."

"I will," Mark replied, "and thank you Olga. Whatever it is

you have done for him, I shall always be grateful." They held each other's gaze for a few moments, before Olga turned away silently and walked back into the plane. Her thoughts turned to the distasteful Colonel Parov, eagerly awaiting her return.

Mark turned to face his son, now inundated with the affection of Julie and his grandparents, all contorting their necks as they told Max how much they loved him. Mark let this continue before a few moments, basking in the unbridled joy of a shattered family now reunited.

Eventually and reluctantly, Mark broke up the party. "Come on son, let's get you home."

81

RISE AGAIN

They had received their orders and were commanded to atone for their previous failures. They were now practically inseparable, and united in purpose. Ever since the *Hawley-Moore Belle* was lost, they had been allowed periodic classified briefings, and had been instructed to be ready to activate their plans as soon as the word was given. From the day of the Russian press conference, they had monitored the Maxwell Anderson situation intently, calculating, patient, waiting for the right time to make their move.

82

WORLD WITHOUT END

Mark and Julie had an agonising wait before they could take Max home. The officials at the airfield gently but firmly explained that Max must first of all undergo debriefing. A secure facility at an undisclosed location had been prepared for this purpose. Trying to be objective, Mark could see that a British citizen returning from two years in Russian captivity, in direct contact with covert facilities and institutions, must tell the security services everything they know. The Cold War was, apparently, alive and well, notwithstanding the Russian Government's conciliatory intentions that inspired Max's release. However, he could not help but feel sorrow for yet another stressful experience for his son, and sanity-testing frustration at a maddening delay in the process of getting to know him again. A painful rehabilitation lay ahead, Mark was certain of that. Putting Max through a potentially traumatic interrogation could only make this harder.

All five of them – Roger and Shirley were also inextricably embroiled – were required to stay in a safe house location in North London for about twenty-four hours. It seemed pointless to resist. To the outside world the building looked like an ordinary end-terrace house. In fact the structure was connected to the rest of the terrace through a network of corridors and purpose-built chambers and ante-rooms in what was a highly sophisticated operations centre, hiding in plain sight. The living quarters were comfortable in a cheap chain hotel kind of way. Mark and Julie were allocated separate bedrooms, to his disappointment, and he liked to think that she was similarly frustrated by their separation. In recent days he began to sense that their former rapport was returning.

They were allowed no contact with Max; they could only hope that he was comfortable, and that his questioners were sympathetic to the fact that here was a twelve year old boy, wrenched once again from familiar surroundings, mourning the loss of his beloved Olga, and afforded only a tantalisingly brief reunion with his family.

The poor kid must be going absolutely out of his mind, Mark rued bitterly, and there was absolutely nothing he could do about it. He cried himself to a fitful sleep.

83

SWEET ELATION

BOY GIANT HOME AT LAST
By Mail Reporter, Ian Steele

There were highly emotional scenes yesterday as Maxwell Anderson, the tallest human being in history, was reunited with his family after two years of captivity in Russia.

Presumed drowned in a shipwreck following a botched kidnap attempt, a tragedy that resulted in the deaths of at least thirty people, Maxwell was sensationally revealed to be alive and well at a Moscow press conference last week. Already ten feet tall at the age of ten when he disappeared, TV footage revealed that the now twelve year old Maxwell had grown to an estimated fifteen feet tall, a full six feet above the height of the previous tallest person, Robert Wadlow of Illinois, USA.

It remains to be seen whether this humanitarian gesture by Moscow will impress the international community. Tensions are running high at the United Nations due to Russia's alleged support for rogue African states, and a recent espionage scandal. A crucial debate at the UN Security Council will take place later this month. Meanwhile, many questions are being asked about the circumstances of Maxwell's rescue by a Russian spy ship, and why this was kept secret from the British Government for so long.

Meanwhile, Maxwell was reported to be in good physical health and delighted to be reunited with his father Mark Anderson, family friend Julie Patterson, and grandparents Roger and Shirley Anderson.

Family spokesman, Ralph Perkins, said: "The whole family is overjoyed that Maxwell is now safely back with his loved ones. The family thanks the Russian and British Governments for enabling his safe return. Maxwell himself is fine, tired and emotional following his experiences, and the family requests that he be afforded privacy at this happy but difficult time."

The astonishing news of Maxwell Anderson's rediscovery and continued exceptional growth has sent shockwaves through the scientific world. Many leading commentators were today calling for a proper study of the boy giant's condition. Professor Julian Robins, Chairman of the Biology and Genetics Research Council, said: "What we have here is possibly the most important evolutionary step in the development of mankind since our ancestors descended from the trees two million years ago. We have to understand what is causing this extraordinary condition. Maxwell Anderson has to be studied."

But human rights campaigners were quick to oppose this. Said Isobel O'Neill of the libertarian pressure group Unchained, "This boy has suffered enough from official interference. The last attempt to study him led to mass slaughter and the wrenching of a defenceless young boy from his loving father. He should be allowed to live his life in peace, surrounded by his family."

A Government spokesman said: "We welcome the fact that a missing British citizen has been returned safe and well to his family. The uniqueness of Maxwell's condition is recognised in Government, but the priority for now is ensuring that he is receiving the very best of care."

As Maxwell Anderson was enjoying his first family dinner for over two years, last night it was clear that his story would continue to fascinate and divide public opinion.

Do YOU think scientists should have the right to study Maxwell Anderson? Text YES or NO to 89099. Texts cost 15 pence + normal message rate. Ask bill payer's permission.

84

THE CONFLICT

As Max neared his thirteenth birthday, around eight months after his return to Britain, he was uncommunicative, monosyllabic, socially awkward, and disrespectful towards his father. Being permanently on strong painkillers was undoubtedly affecting his behaviour, and he was displaying all the classic behaviour traits of a young man embarking upon puberty. Although Mark was not happy about Max's surliness, he understood that the natural chemical changes going on in a pubescent's brain had the effect of suppressing that part of the psyche that governs social interaction. He had been a moody teenager himself! Were it not for the fact that Max was three times the size of his father, the situation was perfectly normal.

Mark attempted to give Max as familiar and stable an existence as could possibly be achieved in the circumstances. They were living in the same custom built bungalow, with its ten feet high doors – perfectly adequate when constructed, but now woefully insufficient – but this was the best accommodation available. Although Ralph was back on board managing the media and commercial contracts, food and clothing supplies and so on, the reality was that building yet another new facility, which would have to be at least twice the size, was an unattainable fantasy. Max moved from room to room by sliding on his knees, which soon wrought havoc with his custom made trousers; the suppliers had begun to complain.

Christine Sullivan, still mousy, all curly hair, once again with thick glasses and dowdy outfits, having apparently eschewed her smarter look, had been re-engaged as Max's tutor and companion. She was the one person whose company he seemed to be comfortable with. Academic studies were not high on the agenda. They played chess, and he taught Christine some Russian. She soothed his burgeoning hormones and pre-teenage angst with musical appreciation sessions. Bucking the trend of most kids Max's age, it was classical music that captured his imagination the most, especially popular suites like The Planets, Peter and the Wolf and Pictures at an Exhibition.

Best of all for Mark during this time was the rekindling of his relationship with Julie. Sharing in their love for Max, she was desperately keen to assist his smooth reintegration, and realised that her presence was a stabilising factor. Late one evening, a couple of months after their stay in the safe house, they were having a particularly difficult day with Max. Badly missing Olga, refusing to speak or eat, he had thrown a plate of food against the wall and angrily barricaded himself into his room, from which the sound of items being broken emanated in between the sobbing, only stopping when Max had raged himself to sleep. Mark's inability to provide the emotional reassurance and empathy his son badly needed made him feel spectacularly useless. Seeing that Mark was gaunt, drawn and distracted, Julie's heart melted. She pulled him towards her, just for a hug, to let him know that someone cares, that she knows how difficult life is for him, and that he's doing his best in an impossible situation. In the warmth and cosiness of a cuddle, it soon became clear to Mark and Julie that they still enjoyed a mutual attraction. Their coupling that night was intense and joyous, providing the cathartic release that only a familiarity with one another's physical needs and peccadilloes could bring. Emotionally vulnerable, distressed and desperate, Mark's primordial sexual responsiveness was stirred by Julie's skilful lovemaking, and he experienced the strongest climaxes of his life.

Some weeks after that glorious joining together, Mark and Julie, searching for ways to make up for the lack of effective human interaction, talked with Max about getting another dog for him, maybe another Dalmatian. This provoked a distressed state in Max, who was still badly traumatised by Matthew's death and guilt-ridden by his own role in that tragedy. No amount of Russian-style psychotherapy was able to cleanse him of this. Spat out through bitter, choking tears, Max made clear that there was no way he ever again wanted to risk having to lose someone he was close to. In addition to the loss of Matthew, his separation from Olga was still an open wound. Mark worried that Max would never allow himself to get close to another person.

Not even his own father.

85

CROSSING OVER

Olga Metovsky shuddered with despair. A messenger was informing her that she was required in the Comrade Colonel's office, or Parov's lair as she had come to think of it. He was getting brazen now, no longer secretive about their frequent assignations. Parov's sexual exploitation of Olga, his price for allowing her to escort Maxwell to England, had recommenced as soon as she returned. Blowing him was now a daily occurrence, and sometimes more than once a day. Her humiliation was abject and his power over her was complete: his influence within the Government machine was such that the consequences of her resistance, or any indiscretion, would be profoundly damaging not just for her life and career, but also for her family, and her beloved father in particular. In recent days Parov had become rougher, pulling her hair hard, making her gag and retch. The names he called her were vile and degrading.

More nervous than usual, she approached his austere oaken door with trepidation, and knocked four times, the agreed signal. Parov opened the door himself, a lop-sided, lustful grin on his face. Short for a Russian colonel, he was no taller than Olga. About fifty, flecks of grey in his close-cropped receding hair, there was the usual faint aroma of body odour around him, probably from the army uniform crumpled around his body, badly in need of laundering.

He gently closed the door and clicked the lock into place. "Kneel, whore," he hissed, and fumbled at his fly.

"Yes, Comrade Colonel Parov," she meekly replied, obedient and respectful just as he liked it.

Olga adopted her customary position next to his oversized mahogany desk. Her knees were sore on the hard wood-panelled floor. He stood over her, exultant, offering himself impatiently. Unable to face him, Olga yelped as he grabbed her red hair, yanking her head upright. "Swallow this, bitch," he growled.

The fishy smell of unwashed skin and stale urine made Olga's eyes water as she took him in her mouth. He groaned and pulled her hair even tighter. Looking up at him, their eyes locked as she fixed his stare, defiant in her subjugation. Parov's grin returned, revelling in his supremacy.

Abruptly his smirk disappeared as he noticed a sudden steeliness in Olga's expression. For a moment, naked hatred poured from her eyes into his, fixing him like a laser harpoon. Before he had time to realise what was happening, in an instant Olga whipped two short kitchen knives from their secreted position, covertly affixed to the desk leg during their last encounter. Simultaneously she thrust the knives into either side of his torso, rupturing several internal organs, and clamped her teeth down with all the strength she could muster, vicelike and ruthlessly, severing flesh and muscle, irreversibly harmful.

Blood spurted from his wounds as Parov sank to the floor, knives protruding from his sides, and as Olga released him, he looked down in horror at the ruinous remnant of his manhood, pulsing more blood. Contorted in agony, he looked into her eyes one last time, imploringly and disbelieving, then gargled his last breath. Triumphant, she spat the lump of gristly meat onto his inert body.

Reaching for the cyanide capsule in her breast pocket, she thought of Maxwell, smiling fondly at her memories of him. Projecting her love to Max as though telepathic, Olga crushed the small glass cylinder between her teeth, and silky blackness eased her heartache away.

86

THE CHANGE

A few months past his thirteenth birthday, and a few inches past eighteen feet tall, puberty had engulfed Maxwell. As if nature had not piled enough misery onto his massive shoulders, he now had disfiguring acne to contend with, compounded by the embarrassment of unreliable vocal chords and sprouting facial hair, and the humiliation of a raw, emerging and sexual awakening.

It was no longer practical to keep Max properly clothed and shoed. Four X Fashions were no longer in business, unable to sustain long term demand even with their association with the tallest ever person. Despite Ralph's best efforts there was no other manufacturer willing or able to provide new supplies. Shirley's attempts to fill the void were almost laughingly unsuccessful. An improvised loincloth-style garment preserved Max's modesty to a point, but heightened his self-consciousness about his body; and leaving the house was now all but out of the question.

It had been, until that point, a reasonably tranquil February Wednesday. Mark was working on his laptop, attempting to get his head around the household finances. He was trying to make sense of the amount of fees charged by Ralph on his latest invoice, and how this related to the dwindling income from media and commercial sources. Max was in his room with Christine, who was there to conduct some home tuition. The audio-visual muzak of daytime television burbled indefatigably, but Mark was barely aware of it. His mind had long since tuned it out.

Without warning, Mark was jarred from his computations by the violent sound of Max yelling, his words spat with ferocity.

"I'M NOT DOING IT! I TOLD YOU I DIDN'T WANT TO AND I'M NOT GOING TO DO IT!

There was a loud crash and a scream of surprise and pain. Jesus Christ, thought Mark, that's Christine. What the Hell is going on? He bolted from the study and hurtled along the corridor to Max's room. As he approached Max's voice filled the air once more.

"I'm sorry I'm sorry I'm sorry! Didn't mean to! DADDY! HELP!"

Mark burst into the room. Max was sat in the corner, hugging his knees, his face twisted with anguish, eyes focused on the furthest wall. Mark followed his gaze, and immediately drew a sharp intake of breath, instinctively covering his mouth with his hands. Christine, upside-down, legs splayed against the wall, her head and upper torso on the floor, contorted in an unnatural angle. Mark rushed over towards her and recoiled at the bloody pulp of her features. She had obviously been struck with tremendous force.

"Christine! Oh my God!"

"I didn't mean to, Daddy, it was an ACCIDENT!"

The injured woman whimpered and moaned, her mouth blowing bubbles of blood and spittle. Thank Christ, thought

Mark, she's alive! Her body began to slump from the wall, and she began writhing on the floor, dazed, unable to speak.

"Try not to move, Christine – I'll get help," said Mark, and frantically stabbed at his smartphone.

87

OUTSIDE LOOKING IN

Christine had been seriously injured; miraculously, not in a way that was life-threatening. She had sustained a concussion; a broken nose, cheekbone and eye socket; a bruised coccyx, chipped pelvis; a dislocated shoulder and some minor ligament damage to her left knee. With proper care and rehabilitation, the casualty doctors had said, she will eventually make a good recovery - although, her appearance would never quite be the same again, and her body would now have inherent weaknesses to be careful about.

Mark was visiting Christine in hospital. Julie was looking after Max, who had been catatonic and traumatised with guilt over the incident. Slurring her words and struggling with the effort of talking through the wire frame that was holding her face together, Christine explained what had happened.

That day's lessons had apparently begun normally; Max had been captivated by tales of destruction, sacrifice, heroism and liberation experienced by Russian soldiers in the Second World War. It was when Christine moved onto maths that Max's mood darkened. Never a favourite subject of his, on this day he refused to engage with the elementary algebra exercises Christine was attempting to take him through. In her typically unflappable but assertive manner Christine gently insisted. Undetectable, the resentment had built in Max's mind until he could control it no longer, like the pressure in a tectonic plate fault before the unleashing of a violent earthquake. He had exploded in a furious tantrum. Lashing out with his gargantuan fist, the power of his punch shattered Christine's face and propelled her into the wall with punishing force.

"Christine, I'm just so, so sorry. If there's anything I can do..."

"You need to have a talk with your son. "Max just isn't happy, Mark. He's so unhappy about his....appearance. I know that's normal for a teenage boy, but poor Max is acutely aware just how extraordinary his body is."

"But that's nothing new."

"True, but things have got a lot worse. He's clearly missing Olga badly, and he's not getting the social interactions or changes of scene necessary to take his mind off things. I think he's realising that life is never going to get better – he can't see a future. And he's no longer able to control his feelings, and he doesn't know his own strength. He has no idea how dangerous his body can be. The size of him, Mark!"

"What can I do about it, though?" said Mark, deeply aware of his inability to address Max's problems, "surely this is....unsolvable? You know I've tried to get hold of Olga, I've written to the Russian Embassy, the Foreign Office..."

"This is not about writing letters, Mark! You're my boss but you're also my friend, and I have to say to you, it's time you gave your son the fatherly support he badly needs. Talk with him, empathise with him, make sure he knows you care, but above all, give him a reason to live. I know you're not happy either, but you have to snap out of it. You have a duty to young Max!" She flushed around the bruising, not used to making impassioned speeches, or castigating her employers.

Her lips trembled, her wounded features now becoming a mask of tears. "That boy is suffering, and he's a danger to himself and to everyone around him. It's up to you to be a man, and be the father Max so badly needs. It's your job to sort it out. No-one else – you!"

"Yes, but..."

"And whatever happens, Mark, I can be of no more help to you – I won't be returning. I can't trust Max not to hurt me again or even kill me."

Back home, Mark slumped in his chair, stunned at this sudden development, although quickly realising that he should have seen this moment coming. Initially perplexed at the loss of Christine, who had shielded Mark from his responsibilities for so long, Mark soon admitted to himself that she was absolutely right.

88

FATHER OF FORGIVENESS

After pacing the corridor anxiously for an hour, Mark knocked firmly on Max's door, mindful from his own experience that a teenage boy should never be barged in on unannounced.

"Who is it?" croaked an unhappy voice from within.

"It's your Dad, big guy." Mark entered the room and noticed a familiar, stale adolescent smell. Max's immense bulk was stretched out on his back upon the specially made bed, legs dangling off the edge at the knees. His straggly blond hair had not been cut for a few months, or washed for many days, and looked a complete mess. Max was wearing his modesty garment, crudely fashioned from a dining room curtain, and was otherwise naked. The plasma television was on, some mindless chat show, which Max was watching disinterestedly. His computer, almost useless because of his titanic hands' inability to operate mouse or keyboard, lay idle next to several unopened study books. Max's easel stood in one corner, pristine white paper untouched for months. Even faithful old Brackie sat alone and cruelly neglected on the shelf.

Mark switched off the set, causing Max to look across at him with a scowl. Mark noticed an angry red spot on Max's nose.

"We need to talk."

"Don't want to," mumbled Max, averting his gaze, unable to hold eye contact. Probably embarrassed about the spot, thought Mark.

"Christine says you're upset. She's gone." Max's saucer-like eyes visibly wilted, clearly wounded by this news. Mark cursed his own tactlessness. An awkward silence lingered between father and son, replicating the experience of fathers and sons everywhere – but none in history had had to cope with a scenario as overpowering as the one that Mark and Max now faced.

"Max, look at me and listen. You're my son and I love you. I'm your father and I'm your best friend. I would do absolutely anything for you. Julie loves you too, and so does your Grandma and Granddad. We know that you're going through a difficult time, but you don't have to face these things alone. We're all here for you."

Max shrugged his immense shoulders. "It won't make any difference."

"What do you mean, big guy?" If only Mark knew how much his son hated that particular term of endearment!

"Can you make me smaller?"

"Er...well, no, but..."

"Can you stop me growing?"

"No, Max, but it will stop soon of its own accord, it has to, we've discussed that."

"You've been saying that for years but it never does. Can you stop me appearing in the news?"

"Probably not, but Ralph can do his best..."

"He can't stop it, and nor can you. I can't go anywhere or do anything. You can't even get me any clothes, I have to wear this… thing." Max gestured disdainfully at his modesty garment.

"We've tried our hardest, Max, and Grandma has done her best to help."

"She's useless. You're all useless," Max was angry now, his gruff voice now interrupted with sobs, "I know what happened to Robert Wadlow. Can you cure my bone disease? Or stop me getting heart problems?"

"Big guy, everything that can be done will be done, the very best doctors, you know that."

"Robert Wadlow died very young. The same thing's going to happen to me, isn't it?"

"We don't know that – no-one knows for sure what will happen. The world hasn't seen anyone like you before."

"Which means the world doesn't know what to do. I've got no life, no friends, no future. I'll never have a girlfriend. Never have a job. I've got nothing to look forward to."

Unable to come up with effective answers, all Mark could do was reach across to his distraught son, and hugged him as best as he could. "It will be alright, big guy, Daddy's here. Daddy will take care of everything."

Mark, however, realised grimly that Max was speaking the truth. His son really did not have any realistic prospect of a normal or happy life. As he continued to grow, and there was nothing to indicate that this would stop any time soon, Max's condition would become ever more bizarre, distressing, painful and unmanageable. Being completely honest with himself, Mark accepted the fact that his son would never be able to work, love, have sex or enjoy anything resembling a comfortable, normal or private life. The sheer impossibility Mark faced in his role as a father, the hopelessness of coping with Max's physical and emotional needs, pressed down upon him with heavy weight as though he was in a centrifuge chamber. In fact, as the increasingly debilitating condition progressed, Mark knew that Max could only expect pain, suffering and an early death. His own sobs now harmonious with those of his son, Mark pressed his head into Max's chest, and secretly wished that the world would end.

89

MOMENTUM

The man and woman had little in common as individuals; they had vastly different backgrounds and professions, and there was even a significant age gap between them. However, they had been drawn together and united by a common purpose, and determined to pursue their shared goals with a ruthless, calm efficiency.

The couple emerged from the Public Records Office, content with their afternoon's work. Their research had been slow progress at times, but now the last of the jigsaw pieces had slotted into place.

Smiling at each other with non-complacent satisfaction, they headed back to the hotel. There were just a few more arrangements to make. Soon, all the stars would be fully aligned, and they would be ready to act.

90

HELP ME

It took a few days of Mark being sullen and tetchy, with Julie persistently attempting to coax the problem out, for Mark to tell her about the conversation he had had with Max. It was the middle of the night. Julie's forceful resentment about yet another sleepless night caused Mark's resolve to finally break. He replayed every single word and sob.

Max himself had been practically catatonic. Without Christine to distract him, he had barely eaten or done anything except vegetate at the television, not even changing the channel, and his interactions with Mark and Julie were now reduced to monosyllabic, unintelligible mumbles.

Julie held Mark tightly to her body. Allowing himself some momentary succour, he revelled in her warm, soothing nakedness and silky touch of her smooth skin.

Through bitter, stinging tears, his words punctuated by fierce sobs, Mark outlined his thoughts on the situation – the appalling circumstances he and Max were in – and, wracked with guilt and shame, he confessed to Julie his thoughts on how he could help his son.

She listened intently, and shaping her thoughts, she patiently waited for him to regain his composure.

"Mark, I'm totally with you on this. We're the only family he's got. We absolutely have to help him. It won't be easy, and we won't be able to do it by ourselves, but I know exactly what to do."

He felt invigorated by her confidence and support. As she explained her ideas to him, his love for her intensified to a level of devotion only surpassed by his love for his son.

91

SEEDS OF GOLD

Mark and Julie sat together in the living room, silent and deathly pale, clasping each other's hands tightly. It was late on Sunday afternoon, the sunlight just beginning to fade. The calm was disturbed by the guttural purr of a sports car's motor which eased to a gentle stop at the front of the house. They heard footsteps, and Mark rose to welcome their expected visitor.

The door opened to reveal a balding middle aged man, slightly overweight, dressed in a smart blue blazer and garish red trousers. The two men hugged wordlessly, a lifetime's friendship passing between them in that simple, warm-hearted embrace. Julie stood at a discreet length behind, respecting the bond the men shared, and the maelstrom of emotions they must each be feeling.

Eventually, Mark said, "Hello, Freddie. Thank you so much for coming."

"Marky, there's nowhere I'd rather be. How are you, matey?" Without waiting for a reply, he looked over to Julie. "How you doing, sweet cheeks?"

She moved over to him, and she took his hand to hers. "Freddie, you'll never know how much this means to Mark. To both of us."

Freddie gave a supportive smile. "You're welcome, gorgeous. Now, is there any chance of a drink? A bit of Dutch courage?"

"There's some whisky in the kitchen. I'll get us some. We could all do with it."

As Julie left to fetch the drink, Mark and Freddie slumped into armchairs, facing each other.

"How's the young lad, then Marky, if that's not a silly question?"

"If anything, he's even worse than when I spoke with you a couple of days ago. He's completely miserable, and refuses to talk to us. I'm very worried he could get violent any time – and you know what happened to poor Christine. There'd be no stopping him."

"Is he still growing?"

"We think so, but it's hard to tell. It's not been easy to measure him for quite a while." Mark sighed, distracted for a moment, unable to look his friend in the eye.

"And what about you, matey?"

"Not good. Without Julie I'd have gone under ages ago. She's fantastic, Freddie, I just don't know what I'd have done without her." Tears were welling up now. "She's been brilliantly supportive. And totally behind me on this."

"Still damned if you do and damned if you don't, though, Marky. How sure are you about it?"

Mark thought for a moment and inhaled to answer, but Julie interrupted them. "Here's the whisky."

Each lost in their own thoughts, they sombrely drained the warm, smoky liquor from their glasses.

It was Julie who broke the silence. "I still feel you should have called your parents, Mark. They're very fond of Max."

"I don't want to argue about that any more. It's best that they don't know."

"But they'll never forgive us. And Shirley will be absolutely devastated."

"We just couldn't take the risk," said Mark. "It's too late now, anyway." This decision was to spawn a schism that would never heal.

"Marky's right, Jules. We need to keep this simple if we can. Granny and Grandpa will understand. My, that booze hit the spot!"

Mark was suddenly decisive, determined, the emotional part of his brain temporarily disengaged.

"Come on, let's do it."

92

WHAT IS LIFE?

"Max, look who's come to visit! It's Uncle Freddie!" There was artificial jollity in Mark's voice. The three adults were stood in Max's doorway, facing the room. Max, an utterly colossal and imposing presence, was sat cross-legged on the floor, facing the plasma television. A nature documentary was on, elephants sweeping majestically across an African plain. Incredibly, even when sat down, the top of Max's unkempt hair brushed the ceiling. He was naked, apart from his modesty garment. The soles of his bare feet were blackened with dirt, and stale sweat pervaded the air.

Max looked across at Freddie and, dosed up on painkillers, gave him a hazy, intoxicated smile. Mark and Julie exchanged a glance; they had not seen Max smile for a long, long time. He's a handsome lad when he smiles, thought Mark, despite the teenage spots.

Max had always liked Freddie, mainly through being bribed by him with sweets and toys as a younger boy. His visits were always eagerly anticipated, riotous fun as they played together, and his departures always resisted. Even as the intervals between Freddie's visits became longer, the fond memories stayed with Max, and even now, despite all that he had been through, his sense of warmth towards Mark's oldest friend remained strong. Mark, of course, realised this, which was exactly why Freddie was with them at this crucial moment.

Freddie, for his part, did well not to reveal his surprise and horror at the gargantuan form that Max had become. Even in a sitting position, Max towered over them, and Freddie saw immediately what a completely impossible situation his friend had been struggling to cope with. Despite his higher loyalties, he felt thankful to be here, with his friend.

"Hi Freddie!" said Max.

"Hello, young man! How are you mate? I've got something for you!" Freddie produced a Crunchie bar from his jacket, Max's favourite, eagerly accepted and devoured in a single mouthful.

"Wash it down with this, mate," said Freddie, proffering a bottle of Cherry Coke, another favourite, Max chugged it down in a single gulp. Freddie looked across knowingly at Mark, who nodded his silent gratitude.

Freddie pulled over a chair and sat down next to Max. Gesturing at the set, he said, "What are you watching, young man? Animals is it? Do you still paint? I remember some of your old pictures, they were really good!"

Freddie was being brilliant, Mark thought appreciatively. Apart from Olga (Mark and Max still blissfully unaware of her fate), Freddie was the only person on the planet currently capable of breaking the ice with Max and keeping him engaged in idle chit-chat, providing a vital distraction.

"I'm ready," said Julie. She used the remote to mute the television, allowing Mark to fade up the music on the MP3 player. It was Peter and the Wolf. For the next several, crucial minutes, it was important that Max's favourite music should be playing.

Freddie was still prattling away when Max let out an almighty yawn.

"I'm tired, Uncle Freddie. Need to sleep. Sorry."

"That's okay, young man. Best give in to it." Again Freddie looked across at Mark. The tranquiliser, deviously mixed with the Cherry Coke, had taken a little longer than they expected to have its effect. The dosage would have floored a large stallion. Inevitably, the muscle relaxant inexorably permeated through Max's system, and he became semi-conscious, limp and receptive.

Mark thought back over the strife of the last thirteen or so years. The appalling, unexplained death of his beloved wife Michelle. The curious and catastrophic ministrations of Geoffrey Kelly and Richard Crowe. Max being thrown out of primary school. Exposure in the national press. The betrayal of his wife's parents, Max's grandparents, Bob and Bell. The devastating and tragic death of Matthew, Max's beloved Dalmatian. The appalling arrogance and incompetence of the Government in the way that Max was taken to be studied, and allowed to be kidnapped. Two years spent bewildered and lonely in a Russian institution, all the while Mark out of his mind with grief. Being wrenched away from a person he clearly loved and respected, the red haired Olga. The misery of being home with his family, unable to find any comfort. Christine's terrible injuries; Mark's failure to give his son the slightest feeling of hope for the future. The mental torment his poor son had endured was enormous and distressing, and he, Mark, had suffered along with him. Throughout all of these unpleasant and stressful experiences, there had been one constant, gnawing fear – that Max would never stop growing, would never be able to live in peace, would also be in physical, psychological and emotional pain.

With Freddie holding one of Max's arms secure, and Julie the other, Mark took the syringe that Julie had prepared, held the point to Max's neck, and carefully pushed the plunger, sending the neurotoxin directly into his son's circulatory system, to reach the brain and heart in moments.

Blinking away tears, Mark cradled Max's huge head, and ran his hand through the tousled blond mop one last time.

"I love you, Max. Daddy said he would take care of you. No more sadness. Sleep well, my wonderful son."

Max's eyeballs rolled upwards, and his body trembled violently as though having a fit; it took all of Freddie's and Julie's strength to keep him as calm as possible. The soaring strings of Peter's signature tune reached a happy crescendo, and Max was still. Serene and handsome, there was a smile on his broad face.

*

Emerging into the brilliant white daylight, Max shielded his eyes from the Sun, burning brightly directly ahead. Ahead of him a figure was silhouetted against the radiance, then there were two figures, the second one larger. They were waiting for him. Max strode forward, light and buoyant, the lush green grass moist and cool under his feet. As he neared the figures, the luminosity receded and Max was exhilarated to recognise the smaller form. Matthew was sat on his hindquarters, snow white and ebony black, tail whipping back and forth excitedly. Unable to contain himself any longer, he bounded forth and leapt into Max's arms, elated at being reunited with his devoted master. Max wept with joy to see his devoted companion.

Stepping forward out of the sunlight, the larger figure materialised with a ghostly, iridescent aura. Her prettiness magnified, red hair lush and luxuriant, Max tingled with excitement and adoration. Olga reached out to take his hand, ready to lead him on his final journey.

93

THE SEPARATED MAN

BOY GIANT TRAGEDY:
FATHER ARRESTED
By Mail reporter, Ian Steele

In a further dramatic twist to the already fantastic Maxwell Anderson saga, last night police arrested the boy giant's father Mark Anderson with his son's murder.

Mr Anderson, 46, was today being questioned by detectives at an undisclosed location.

Maxwell Anderson, the world's tallest ever person, died last week at the age of only 13. Police have not yet released the cause of death.

Family spokesman, Ralph Perkins, said: "This is a devastating tragedy. The family asks that their privacy be respected at this desperately difficult time."

Mr Anderson's arrest is the latest twist in the extraordinary story of young Maxwell, whose superhuman growth baffled the scientific world. At the time of his death, he was believed to be eighteen feet tall, double the height of the previous record breaking human, Robert Wadlow.

Maxwell's rescue by Russian authorities from a botched kidnapping was indirectly responsible for triggering a thawing of East-West relations. Already the target of an extremist cult, there were growing fears that the death of young Maxwell could spark anti-establishment protests and even mass suicides amongst Maxwell's fanatical followers.

For the latest developments on this unfolding story, please keep checking the Mail's website.

94

CRADLE TO THE GRAVE

The boy swore under his breath as his mother shouted to him up the stairs.

"James! Visitors! Come downstairs please!"

How dare they disturb him – he was so close to completing the final level of Zombie Resurrection IV after weeks of incessant gaming. Didn't they realise he had better things to do than see visitors, whoever the Hell they are? If they didn't want him to play the game, why did they give it to him for his birthday? He flicked his floppy blond fringe out of his eyes and carried on obliterating zombies.

Having just turned fourteen, James was an unhappy teenager. Gangly and spotty, he was constantly and insensitively teased by his parents about hairy palms, to his acute, burning embarrassment. He practically barricaded himself in his bedroom a couple of years ago, reeling from the revelation that his parents were not his real mother and father. He had been adopted as a baby, and for twelve years had been living blissfully unaware that his birth parents had not wanted him, and he was living with a substitute family.

"James! Downstairs, now!"

"All RIGHT!" he yelled, and turned off the console in

disgust. Stomping across the landing and trudging down the stairs, he entered the living room to see his adoptive mother and father with two people he didn't recognise.

The man was in his forties, his greying blond hair very thin now, and with sunglasses perched on his head, a habit he had never been able to break. He was dressed in expensive, designer, smart-casual clothes, his shirt slightly too small for his rotund figure. The woman was younger, slim and athletic looking, with long brown hair. She was smart and officious.

His father said, "James, say hello to your Uncle and Auntie."

James stood silent, confused. He had no idea that he had any relatives. Who were these people?

It was Freddie Abbott who spoke first, in a friendly, engaging voice. "My word, Bob and Bell, what a handsome young man."

Caroline Harris said, "Hello James, we're thrilled to meet you! And my goodness, haven't you grown!"